Augustin Daly, Gustav von Moser

Our English friend

A comedy in 4 acts

Augustin Daly, Gustav von Moser

Our English friend
A comedy in 4 acts

ISBN/EAN: 9783337103569

Printed in Europe, USA, Canada, Australia, Japan

Cover: Foto ©Andreas Hilbeck / pixelio.de

More available books at **www.hansebooks.com**

OUR

ENGLISH FRIEND.

A Comedy in 4 Acts.

BY

AUGUSTIN DALY.

AS ACTED AT DALY'S THEATRE, FOR THE FIRST TIME,
NOVEMBER 25TH, 1882.

NEW YORK:
PRINTED, AS MANUSCRIPT ONLY, FOR THE AUTHOR.
1884.

DRAMATIS PERSONÆ AND ORIGINAL CAST.

PAUL SPENCER, A Young New Yorker, who has migrated to
the enterprising township of Cutty Corners, for the Hunt-
ing Season . . . . MR. JOHN DREW
ELIDA SPENCER, his Wife, entertaining a few city friends in
the country for the first time . . . . . MISS VIRGINIA DREHER
DIGBY DE RIGBY, their English friend, who finds himself,
singularly enough, to be an unexpected guest . MR. JAMES LEWIS
WIRT LAURENS, who has been invited to "come up and shoot"
MR. YORKE STEPHENS
MERRYL LAURENS, his Wife, with the most inattentive hus-
band in the world . . . . MISS HELEN LEYTON
FREDERIC FLUTTERBY, Mixture of the Honeybee and
Butterfly . . . . MR. CLEMENT BAINBRIDGE
MRS. CORNELIA PARTRADGE, an amiable old lady, who
possesses two pretty nieces, who is no sooner comfortably
relieved of one by Hymen, than the other makes things
lively for her . . . . MRS. G. H. GILBERT
BARBIE VAUGHN, the other niece, destined to complete a
conquest begun by her sister . . . . MISS ADA REHAN
ALONZO GROOBIE, Pharmaceutist of Cutty Corners,
MR. E. T. WEBBER
TRIPHENA GROOBIE, his Wife, and leader of the *ton* in Cutty
Corners . . . . MISS MAY SYLVIE
THEOBALD BLUM, Clerk at Groobie's Pharmacy,
MR. WILLIAM GILBERT
JACKSON, Farmer on Spencer's place, with an aversion to Pill-
grinders . . . . MR. WEBBER
MIMA JACKSON, the Farmer's Daughter, and fatal to the peace
of Theobald . . . . MISS MAY FIELDING
UNCLE SPENCER, who is ruthlessly sacrificed to the Spirit of
Hospitality . . . . MR. CHARLES FISHER
JOHN, the Butler . . . . ⎫ . . . . MR. STERLING
NAP, the Help . . . . . ⎬ AT SPENCER'S ⎰ . . . . . MR. BEEKMAN
SARAH, Housemaid . . . ⎭ ⎱ . . . . . MISS HAPGOOD

THE TIME—The Present.
THE PLACE—Cutty Corners, in Northern New York.
THE SCENE—Reception Hall and General Room at Spencer's
Country House.

. ACT I.

SCENE—*General hall in Paul Spencer's country house, at Cutty
Corners, Northern New York. Everything of a light, airy,
summery character, quite of the decorative order, however.*
at C. *a stairway leads up straight, and then to an upper door, in* R.
flat. R. *of stairs, in back wainscotting, a closet.*
Two doors at R. *between which is a mantle-piece. Arch at* R. U. F.
L. *of* C. *is a vestibule with double doors at back, opening in upon the
stage.*
L. *of vestibule, at back, a window, with a view of lawn and country
beyond.*
At L. H. *a door and window, between which is a cabinet.*
L. U. E. *a large semi-circular arch with broad steps, leading to a
library.*

The curtain rises to a lively air, discovering NAP *and* JOHN *bringing a sofa down stairs, directed by* SARAH.

Nap. Golly, this sofia heavy. Whar de sofa to go, Miss
Sarey?
Sarah. [*Pointing down* L.] Down there. Don't back into
those vases! Mind the chair! Look out for that pedestal! Oh
dear, dear, the clumsiness of these creatures!
Nap. [*Crosses to* R., *wiping his forehead.*] It's wuss dan
makin hay when de sun shines.
John. [L.] Shall I bring in the step ladder for the curtains?
Sarah. [*Back of sofa.*] No, Miss Mima will attend to that.
My lady farmer's daughter orders things just as she wants 'em,
in this house. But I suppose, as it's Mrs. Spencer's first summer
at country housekeeping, she's glad of any help she can get.
John. [*Down* C.] Well, we mustn't be too hard on a bride.
Oh! Here she is.

. LIDA SPENCER *and* MIMA *enter*, R. 2 D.

Lida. There, I leave all that for you. You do everything so
well.
Mima. [*Handing some lace curtains to Sarah.*] Here, take
these up to the pink room. [SARAH *goes up-stairs.*] Nap, you

get the steps. John, you help him, quick! quick! [*They all scamper off.*]

Sarah. [*On the stairs.*] One would think she was the lady of the house, with them airs. [*Exits* R. C., *up-stairs.*]

Lid. [*Going to cabinet,* L.] We never shall have everything ready. [*Taking out silver.*] The more we do, the more I find we have forgotten.

Mim. Oh, we'll be ready. [*Arranging mantle.*] In ten minutes you can sit down in comfort, and wait for the folks to come.

Lid. I shan't sit down once in comfort, till they're gone.

Mim. Talking of comfort, we do want a sofa dreadfully for that room. [*Pointing off,* R. 1 E.]

Lid. [*Forward.*] We havn't got a sofa, so that's off my mind.

Mim. I know of one—uncle's—up in the library.

Lid. Mr. Spencer's uncle? I wouldn't dare to ask him.

Mim. I would. He can only say no.

Lid. [*Suddenly.*] Hush! [*Listens.*] Somebody coming up the walk.

Mim. [*Listening, up to window.*] I think I hear two bodies.

Lid. It can't be callers. That would be dreadful just now, when we're expecting a house full of people.

Mim. It would be like these stupid country folks!

Lid. It can't be any of our friends—the train's not in.

Mim. No—I'm betting on villagers.

GROOBIE and MRS. GROOBIE *outside,* L. C., *visiting costume; loud country effect.* MIM. *and* LID. *are at* L.

Mim. [*Peeping.*] It is—

Lid. Who? [MRS. G. *pulls door bell, at vestibule outside.*]

Mim. The Groobie's.

Lid. The what?

Mim. Groobie's—keep the drug store.

Lid. Oh, horrors!

Mim. You run away. I'll get rid of them.

Lid. No, we must be polite to the village people. I'll call Mr. Spencer. [*Darts out,* R. 2 D. *Bell.*]

NAP *appears,* L. U. E., *to answer bell, opens vestibule door,* L. C., *and admits* MR. *and* MRS. GROOBIE.

Mim. And I'll disappear. [*Darts up-stairs,* R. C.]

Nap. [L., *to Mrs. Groobie.*] Yes, 'm. What name, ma'am?

Mrs. Groobie. [*With dignity to Groobie.*] A card, Alonzo!

Groobie. [R., *lank, spectacled, ill at ease, badly-fitting clothes.*] Yes, my love. There! [*Hands card to Nap.*] Are you quite well? [*Crosses to* C.]

Nap. Well, just so so, sah.

Gr. You don't look well. You are pale. [*Crosses to* R.]

Nap. Golly Mass' Groobie, when I git pale, I'se done for.

Mrs. G. [c.] Don't detain the man. [*Sees the card.*] Heavens, what on earth have you done, Alonzo! A business card with a list of your drugs! Do you want to sicken the people at the very first? [*Snatches the card from Nap.*]

Gr. [R.] Drugs are to cure people, my love, not to sicken them. However! [*Takes the card back and searches his pockets.*] I guess I forgot the others.

Mrs. G. Alonzo, this is dreadful! Our first call and no cards!

Gr. Well, that ain't the only dreadful thing about it. [*Still searching.*] My boots are so tight, they draw tears to my eyes.

Mrs. G. Don't keep the man waiting.

Gr. [*To Nap.*] All right, you know us. Trot along.

Mrs. G. [*With dignity.*] Say that Mr. and Mrs. Groobie have called.

Nap. [L.] Yes, 'm, I know the name. [*Aside, crossing up to* c.] De paregoric and the gum drop store. [*Exits,* R. 2 D.]

Mrs. G. Sit down, Alonzo. Don't stand there like a scarecrow. [*Sits* L.]

Gr. I feel like one every time I put on these clothes. I say, you forgot to let the coat out under the arms. I told you last Sunday, in church, it was too tight; I couldn't get a wink of sleep. [*Sits.*]

Mrs. G. [*On sofa,* L.] Don't perch on the edge of the seat.

Gr. If I sit back, something will split when I get up,—and I can ease my boots this way.

Mrs. G. [*Savagely.*] I declare you are the most—[*Rising and sweetly to* LIDA, *who enters,* R. 2 D.] Ah, my dear Mrs. Spencer, how delighted I am to find you at home; we took the opportunity of paying our respects. [*Stops short.*]

SPENCER *enters, followed by* NAP, R. 2 D., NAP *exits,* L. C.

Lida. Mr. Spencer, Mr. and Mrs. Groobie; our neighbors, Paul!

Spencer. [R. C., *shakes hands with Groobie.*] How do you do? [*Bows to Mrs. G.*] Happy to see you.

Lid. [*Going to sofa.*] I'm sorry you find us in some disorder. We are expecting company by the train, and this is my first summer housekeeping. So we are full of preparation.

Gr. [*Rising.*] Then I guess we'd better be going.

Lid. Pray, don't, Mr. Groobie. I should be very sorry.

Mrs. G. [*Cheerfully and sweetly.*] Sit down, Alonzo, dear. You mustn't guess things, darling. [*To Lid.*] There's nothing he hates so much as paying visits. But I know what expecting company is. It's just one run for days before, and nobody to help. My husband never helps a bit. Alonzo, I'm sure Mr. Spencer don't leave everything to his wife, as you do.

Sp. [R.] Oh, I assure you I'm much worse than Mr. Groobie.

Gr. There, Triphena!

Mrs. G. [*Speaks with frequent pauses in hopes that Lid. will talk.*] I don't believe a word of it. What a pretty place you've made of this old rookery. [*Pause.*] Just like our house. All the new style. [*Pause.*] Teagreen walls—ebony mouldings—mahogany—[*pause*]—all except Groobie's study, that's drab, because he smokes so much—[*pause.*] Nasty habit, but I'll cure him. [*Pause.*] Does your husband smoke?

Lid. Yes. [*Trying to hide her impatience.*]

Mrs. G. [*Same business as above.*] Of course, I like the smell of a good cigar, but Groobie smokes a pipe. [*Pause.*] We haven't given our housewarming yet. [*Pause.*] I'm glad of it, since you've come to stay all summer. [*Pause.*] But mercy on me, I'm talking away, and you are busy. We must take our leave. [*All rise.*]

Lid. [*Aside, gets L.*] Thank goodness.

Sp. [*To Gr., getting C.*] Do you shoot?

Gr. Shoot? Shoot what?

Sp. I mean, are you much of a sportsman?

Mrs. G. Of course you are, Alonzo. Didn't I work a game bag for you?

Gr. Oh, yes. [*To Sp., aside.*] A game bag with yellow ground, and red birds flying away from a green pointer! How do you think the game would like that bag?

Mrs. G. [*To Sp.*] He *is* a sportsman.

Sp. I'm glad to hear that. We shoot to-morrow and next day—start at night, so as to be on the spot bright and early. I shall be glad to have you with us.

Lid. [*To Mrs. G.*] We dine after their return—so, if you will help me to receive the weary hunters after their day's sport—

Mrs. G. [*Sitting. All sit, rapturously.*] With pleasure. Alonzo, you can trust young Blum in the shop all day, can't you?

Gr. It's risky. [*To Sp.*] I never saw a man handle deadly poisons like that young chap, and so overconfident! He weighs out drugs, as if he were serving sugar, and a couple of lumps made no difference.

Mrs. G. [*Snappishly.*] Well, it don't. [*To Lid.*] I must ask you, as you're just from the city—it just reminds me—[*confidentially*]—how do they dress for a shooting dinner? High neck or *decolleté.*

Lid. Oh, very plainly.

Mrs. G. I'm sorry for that. Low neck becomes me so! What a bother dressing is, isn't it?

Lid. It is, particularly when you expect a train every minute, and havn't begun yet.

Mrs. G. I declare, we must go. [*Rises—all rise and shake hands.*] But I'm so glad to have found you at home. There, I forgot the chief thing. [*Sits—they all sit.*] You must give me your advice. Of course we call on you, because Mr. Spencer's people always had a place here, and you will come every summer; so you—so to speak—are one of us. But there are some people, who took cottages only for the season, and seem very nice. Now, ought we to call? Mr. Groobie, as it were, represents the village; everybody looks up to him—he knows, you see, pretty much all their complaints, and, if the village ought to recognize these people, we must lead the way.

Gr. [*Looks at watch—rises.*] My dear, we are really detaining our friends.

Mrs. G. [*Rises—all rise.*] Then I won't say another word. [*To Lid., affectionately.*] We'll talk it over quietly, to-morrow. Come, Alonzo

Gr. [*Shaking hands with Sp.*] All right, my dear.

Mrs. G. [*Returning, in confidence to Lid., and bringing her front.*] Isn't Groobie a model? [SP. *sits,* GR. *goes up angrily.*] Your husband seems just as obedient. But that's the way for young wives: train your husband the first year, or you'll never do it. Now, Alonzo. [*Rises.*]

Gr. Are you quite sure you're going?

Mrs. G. Oh, quite. Good-bye, Mr. Spencer. [*Crossing from one to the other, dodges to get by.*] Good-bye, Mrs. Spencer. [*Shakes hands.*]

Sp. and Lid. Good-bye.

Mrs. G. [*Volubly, as all go to door,* C.] Now don't come to the door. We know you must be in a great hurry. Trains don't stop for any one—and when the train's in, the people are right on top of you. I tell Mr. Groobie that trains are like death. They come when you don't want them, and they're awful slow when you're waiting. Now don't come one step further. Alonzo, dear, your arm. Good-bye. [*Exeunt* GR. *and* MRS. G. SP. *and* LID. *throw themselves into opposite chairs.*]

Sp. Whew!

Mrs. GROOBIE *returns.* *They rise.*

Mrs. Groobie. So silly of me, I left my parasol. Oh, here it is. A birthday present from Groobie. I would not lose it for the world.

GROOBIE *returning, in doorway.*

Groobie. My dear—
Mrs. G. [Sp. *thinking to shake hands with her, takes hold of her parasol, as they turn up stage.*] Coming, love. Good-bye, again, good-bye! [*Exits, C. L.*]
Sp. [*Crossing to* LID., *who sits disconsolate.*] Don't look so distressed. It's all over. [*Holds her head up, standing behind her, and bends down to kiss her.*]
Lid. [*Disengaging, crosses* R.] Some one's coming.
Mim. [*Peeping over the bannisters,* R.] Here's Uncle Joyce; now for his sofa. [*Comes down.*]
Sp. You're not going to rob the old gentleman?
Lid. It's not my doing. Mima's the conspirator. [*Exit,* R. 2 D. MIM. *runs down, looks about her, sees Unc.'s hat on table,* R., *and drops it behind stairs, then hides behind staircase.*]
Mim. Now for him.

UNCLE JOYCE SPENCER *enters down stairs,* R. C.

Sp. [*Aside to Mim.*] Now don't impose on him, mind! I won't have it. [*Exits,* R. 2 D.]
Mim. [*Watching* UNC., *who rummages about, searching, aside.*] He seems in a very bad humor. [*Aloud.*] Are you looking for anything in particular, sir? [*Coming down.*]
Uncle. [R.] Am I looking for anything in particular? Do I look as if I were looking for nothing in particular? I'm trying to find my hat. I could solemnly swear I put it down here. [*Looks.*]
Mim. No wonder it got lost.
Unc. What's that?
Mim. [*Gets hat from behind stairs.*] I've got it. [*Hides it behind her as she approaches him.*] What will you give me for it?
Unc. [R.] Come, come, no nonsense. Give me my hat.
Mim. You must promise what I ask.
Unc. Mima, you're too big to play spoiled child any longer.

Mim. What a fuss about an old hat! Didn't I say I'd give it, if you gave me something in return? And besides, who spoiled me? Didn't papa tell you a hundred times I'd never grow up to be any good, if you didn't teach me to keep my place—and didn't you take me on your lap and tell him he couldn't appreciate such a creature?

Unc. How the toad remembers!

Mim. But he does appreciate me, and I'm going home with him, and I'll never set foot in this house again. [*Going* c.]

Unc. Will you kindly leave my hat behind?

Mim. I cannot. I said I'd give it on one condition.

Unc. In the name of goodness, why don't you say what you want, then?

Mim. I'm waiting to be asked. Please recollect you havn't asked me yet. [*Comes down, puts his hat on his head, arranging it on his head, going up and down to adjust it.*] I'm as reasonable as anybody, when people talk reason. There! that will do. [*Crosses to* R.] Now you are beginning to smile. How a smile becomes that hat! It isn't a hat to get mad under! Now, can I have your sofa?

Unc. [L.] My sofa!

Mim. Yes, your sofa, out of the library—to put in there [*Points* R.] for company.

Unc. Well, upon my word!

Mim. Upon your word! All right. Mind, I've got your word on it. Remember your promise.

Unc. I promised nothing.

Mim. Give me back the hat, then. [*Tries to get at it. He takes her hands.*]

Unc. You shall have the sofa. It was not necessary to resort to stratagem. My nephew's friends are welcome to all I possess.

Mim. Humbug!

Unc. How dare you?

Mim. You know you do it all for my sake. I'm too big to sit on your knee, but you may kiss me. [UNC. *does so. She curtsies.*] Thank you. You'll miss the sofa very much.

Unc. [*Stage* L.] Never! Don't mention it. [*With a grimace.*]

Mim. It was very comfortable as a sofa, but as a good action, it will make you more comfortable still. [*Exits,* L. U. E.]

Unc. The spoiled pixie. [*Going up.*]

SPENCER *enters,* R. 2 E.

Spencer. Going out, uncle? How about your *siesta?*

Unc. How the dickens can a man sleep in a house upside

down? I'll take a trot outdoors, and come back prepared to give up my bed, and sleep in a hammock. [*Exits,* c.]

Sp. [*Calling after him.*] Don't be long. Train's overdue now.

LIDA *enters, dressed,* R. 2 D.

Lida. Oh, you're there. Where did Mima go?

MIMA *enters from library, meeting* NAP *and* JOHN *from* L. C.

Mima. This way. [*Up stage.*] This way. [*They ascend steps to library.*] We'll have it here in a minute.

Lid. Poor uncle!

Mim. We had a battle. I won it, and now I'm going for the spoils. [*Exits,* L. U. E., *with* NAP *and* JOHN.]

Sp. [*Puts his arms around Lida's waist.*] Now, everything is in order, take a moment's comfort.

Lid. I can't. I'm not nearly through. There's somebody coming. [*Crosses to* L.]

Sp. [*Holding her.*] No, there's not. I'm not nearly through, either.

Lid. Now, what do you want?

Sp. First—only a kiss.

Lid. I havn't a moment's time.

Sp. Very well. Take your time. I can wait.

JACKSON *appears at* L. C.

Lid. There is somebody. [*Breaks away, crosses to* R.] Good afternoon, Jackson. [*To Sp.*] I told you. [*Exits,* R. 2 D.]

Jackson. Good afternoon.

Sp. Oh, Jackson. I sent for you to ask whether you found any partridges yesterday.

Jack. Plenty, sir. Woods full of 'em.

Sp. We shall have lots of company, and they'll want the best sport we can give them.

Jack. We can give them something first-rate, sir.

Sp. You remember Mr. Laurens. He went out with us last year.

Jack. Oh, he was a good one. I'll be bound he's come for fun. We made a good bag with him, sir.

LIDA *re-enters,* R. 2 D., *as* MIMA *re-appears* L. U. E., *followed by* JOHN *and* NAP, *carrying lounge, which they take off,* R. 1 E. *Return and exeunt* L. C.

Lida. Your daughter is really invaluable, Jackson. She takes all the trouble off my hands.

Jack. [L.] Well, she's been treated pretty well up here, ma'am, and she ought to do something for it. But I guess I'll have to take her home a bit, for to keep house for me.

Lid. [R.] I can give her an excellent character as house-keeper.

Mima. [*Returns from seeing sofa off,* R. 1 E., *pats Jack.'s cheek.*] You dear old papa.

Jack. Behave yourself. I'm busy now.

Sp. Have Peter and one or two boys ready at five to-morrow, Jackson. How is Juno? Got over her trouble?

Jack. Famous, sir, and wild for the birds. Is that all, sir?

Sp. ⋅ That's all, Jackson.

Jack. Now, come along, you baggage. Step out—one—two—one—two.

Mim. One—two—one—two. [*Exeunt, laughing and keeping step,* R. U. E.]

Sp. Now, have you a moment to attend to your poor husband?

Lid. [R.] Paul, you know I never neglect you, but so many people are coming.

Sp. If I had thought of giving you so much trouble, I could have invited one at a time.

Lid. Oh, it's better to have them all at once, and be over with it. It would be all right, but for two things.

Sp. Specify the difficulties.

Lid. First—Sister Barbie. That girl has such a will of her own.

Sp. Your Aunt Cornelia comes with her, and may be safely trusted to manage the young lady. Your Aunt Cornelia knows what she's about. She married you off, you know.

Lid. Oh, yes, but Barbie is not the weak-minded creature that I was! She won't take the first man that offers, to oblige her aunt.

Sp. Ahem! let us pass on to the second difficulty.

Lid. The second difficulty is Aunt Cornelia herself. I'm afraid of her.

Sp. [L.] Why afraid of the harmless, necessary aunt?

Lid. You men can't understand. A young housekeeper of only a year's experience stands in dread of these veterans. She'll pick us all to pieces.

Sp. Have no fear, darling, and all will be well.

Lid. Don't you think I've managed everything nicely? [*Goes to* L. D.] This is for Mr. and Mrs. Laurens. [*Pushes door open.*]

Sp. Decorated *à la chinoise.* Very pretty.

Lid. The spare room up-stairs is for Mr. Flutterby, and these [*Goes to* R. 1 E.] are for aunt and Barbie.

Sp. [L.] Capitally arranged.

Lid. [*Crosses to* L.] And that takes up every corner of the house. If a mouse were to pay us a visit, we havn't a cupboard to put him into.

Sp. I say, what if our friend De Rigby were to pop in on us?

Lid. Mr. De Rigby! Heavens! you don't expect him? I thought he wasn't coming!

Sp. I suppose not, but he didn't give me a positive answer, when I asked him down for the shooting. We don't know what may happen.

Lid. [*Resolutely.*] If he comes, I give up. I shan't know what on earth to do!

Sp. Poor fellow! He was very fond of you—before our marriage, you know.

Lid. But think of our predicament! Why, I had to give my dressing-room to Aunt Cornelia.

Sp. Oh, a man can be stowed anywhere—on a billiard table.

Lid. But, my love, we havn't another bed! Would you like me to sleep in a trunk?

Sp. [R.] I was only joking. Rigby certainly won't come, without letting us know.

Lid. I declare you frightened me. I sincerely trust he's safely back in England before this. [*Crosses to* R.]

Sp. At this moment he is probably at the sea-side, making love to some fair mermaid, and just as I found him making love to you at Brighton, when I carried you off before his very eyes. You know, making love is his weakness. It's the standing joke against him.

NAP *enters quickly, smiling all over,* L. C.

Nap. Golly, Mass Spencer—He's just a drivin' up, sah!

Sp. Who's just driving up?

Nap. Mr. De Rigby.

Lid. [*Sinks in chair,* R.] Oh, heavens!

Sp. Go down to the gate, and bring up his luggage.

Nap. Yes, sah! Golly, I'se glad Mass Rigby come! [*Exits,* L. C.]

Lid. [*Anxiously, starting up.*] What on earth shall we do?

Sp. It's awful, but it can't be helped.

Rigby. [*Outside.*] All right, Nap.

Lid. There he is. [*Runs out,* R. 2 D.]

RIGBY *enters, followed by* NAP, *carrying gun-case, valise and hat-box,* L. C.

Rigby. Here I am, old boy! What do you say to this, for a surprise?

Sp. [R., *shaking his hand warmly.*] I'm glad to see you.

Rig. Didn't write purposely. Wanted to spring it upon you.

Sp. You have sprung it admirably.

Rig. I'm glad to hear it. Would have come to see you long ago, old fellow, but couldn't manage to get off for longer than a day. Now I've got two weeks at least, and can settle down comfortably with you—that is, if it's no inconvenience.

Sp. [*Glancing after his wife.*] Not in the least. Make yourself at home.

Rig. Thank you. [*Takes off hat, gloves, etc.*]

Nap. Whar shall I put de things, sah?

Sp. Hm! ask Mrs. Spencer.

Nap. She told me to ax you, sah.

Sp. [*Confused.*] Well, put them down for the present.

Nap. Yes, sah—dey is dere already, sah! [*Exits,* C. L.]

Rig. [*Looks round.*] Nice place. Capital arrangements.

Sp. [R.] , Yes, the house is unfortunately rather small. It's all on this floor, except a couple of attic closets up-stairs.

Rig. What of that? Old friends don't mind a little cramping; so, if it's all the same, I'll take my attic at once. [*Goes to glass.*] Beastly driving over here. Jolly nasty climate you've got! Which way do I go? [*Crosses to* R.]

Sp. Well—ah—wait and see Mrs. Spencer before you go—to —your room.

Rig. [*Surveys himself.*] I'd rather make up a bit before I meet her. I'm a little ruffled. Got out at the wrong station, and had to drive over in a wagon. Roads were damnable, as the theologians say. By the way, old fellow, I had quite an adventure.

Sp. Indeed! Was she pretty? You're as soft as ever.

Rig. Not soft at all. If you had seen her foot! It was the first glimpse I had of her, as she got off the train—then her walk! Not a vulgar, solid, female tramp, but a floating—a skimming— an undulating—

Sp. [C.] Yes, yes, I know!

Rig. [R.] And that foot and walk belonged to a creature! I—I never beheld anything so perfect! Oh, my dear fellow, she was a corker! What a woman—tall, slender, *distinguée*—how shall I describe her? I tell you, a being produced by nature regardless of cost. [*Crosses to* L.]

Sp. Poor fellow! Same Digby de Rigby!

Rig. No. I no longer fall in love with every pretty face. I have, however, acquired a true sense of the really beautiful.

Sp. Same thing.

Rig. [*Sits on sofa,* L.] To return to my adventure. I was absorbed in contemplation of her form and movements, when suddenly she raised her veil!

Sp. That settled you.

Rig. To use a cant expression—I was "off."

Sp. Describe her matchless features!

Rig. She was a blonde. You know, I have a weakness for blondes. When she finally moved away—

Sp. You followed.

Rig. No, I was insensibly drawn after.

Sp. Same thing, same result.

Rig. I had the good fortune to pick up her satchel. She thanked me. I dexterously opened—

Sp. The satchel?

Rig. A conversation. She talked with greatest readiness. Not a bit of diffidence. Wonderful, you know. I secured her a seat in waiting room—brought her a cup of tea—received the sweetest of thanks, and began to walk in the clouds?

Sp. [R.] Your favorite walk.

Rig. In the midst of my happiness, another party interposed. A threatening, fiery female bore down upon us—the very reverse of the pretty little craft I had spoken. In fact, as the mariners say, a perfect piratical old hulk.

Sp. [R.] I suppose you mean by that, a respectable, well-behaved, elderly lady, with no nonsense about her.

Rig. Not a nonsense! Of course, she thanked me for my attentions to her niece, and then engrossed the conversation. I couldn't get another word with the angel. The aunt seemed bound to find out who I was, and where I was going. I paid her off with a plumper, told her I travelled for a champagne house— Duc de Montebello—and was drumming the neighborhood.

Sp. Very neat and ready. Did she swallow it?

Rig. To use an ornithological expression—like a magpie.

Sp. And dropped you immediately?

Rig. To borrow a culinary illustration—like a hot potato. She whisked her niece off, at the double quick. But here I am chattering, when I ought to be brushing up.

Sp. [*Uneasily.*] You look very well.

Rig. [*Looks at his clothes.*] It's a capital suit for travelling, but it won't do for the ladies. So, old fellow, if you don't mind— where is my room? [*Up stage.*]

Sp. [R.] Wait till Nap comes to carry your things.

Rig. No, no, I'm an old campaigner and help myself. [*Picks up all his things and stands waiting with his eyeglass in his eye.*]

Sp. [*Aside.*] There's no help for it, I must give him a place somewhere. [*Aloud.*] Well, if you *will* have it. [*Opens door,* L.] Here you are.

Rig. [*Looks in.*] Charming! It's really too fine! Bouquets, flowers! Well, old fellow, this is what I call a reception! [*Shakes hands.*] This is friendly! [*Drops his hat-box.* SP. *picks it up, and pushes him off with it. Exits,* L. 1 E.]

Sp. Try and make it do. [*Closes door.*] Where can I possibly stow him, when they put him out of that?

LIDA *enters,* R. 2 D.

Lida. I'm so glad, dear, you're alone. I've thought it all over; you had better tell Mr. de Rigby candidly, that he can't stay.

Sp. That's impossible, my love.

UNCLE JOYCE SPENCER *enters,* R. C., *down stairs.*

Uncle. Here are your guests—all at the gate.

Lid. [*Nervously to Sp.*] But Paul!

Sp. It would be foolish, absurd. [*Exits,* L. C.]

Lid. [*Calls after him.*] But what shall we do? Dear, dear! [*Comes down* C.]

Unc. [R.] What's the matter, daughter?

Lid. [*Tearfully.*] Paul shows such a want of consideration for my feelings!

Unc. Can't be. He adores you.

Lid. Then he shouldn't be so abrupt. But you always take his part. I'm used to that. [*Crosses to* R.]

Unc. Very good; she takes my sofa, then blows me up. We are having a good deal in one day.

SPENCER *enters,* L. C., *with* MERYL LAURENS *on his arm, followed by* LAURENS *and* FLUTTERBY, *the latter carrying a lady's hat-box and shawl.*

Meryl. [*Running to Lid. and kissing her.*] My dear Lida!

Lid. My dear Meryl! [*Shakes hands with Lau.*] I'm so glad to see you! [*Shakes Flut.'s hand.*] How do you do, Mr. Flutterby?—Uncle—Mr. Flutterby!

Unc. [*Who has already shaken hands with the others.*] Happy to make your acquaintance! [*Shakes hands.*]

Flutterby. It was so good of you to remember me! [LID. *and* MER. *converse at* R., UNC. *and* FLUT. *just above them,* R. LAU. *comes down with* SP., L.]

Laurens. [L. C.] So, there's good shooting.

Spencer. [L.] Saved it all for you.

Lau. I've quite longed for this visit, though we've had no end of luck ourselves. Bagged two hundred woodcock last week. I've been out every day, except four rainy ones.

Mer. [R., *calling her husband.*] Wirt!

Lau. [*Not heeding.*] My new gun is a marvel. It reminds me of that muzze-loader I used to carry—old never-fail!

Mer. [*Calling impatiently.*] Wirt, dear!

Lau. This is the first breech-loader I ever carried, that gave me satisfaction. I know we've got to like them, and all that.

Mer. Wirt!

Flut. [*Crossing to Lau.*] I beg your pardon, but Mrs. Laurens is calling you.

Mer. [*To Flut.*] Thank you.

Flut. Don't mention it.

Lau. [*To Mer.*] What is it, my darling?

Mer. Are you sure all our things were put off?

Lau. Quite, darling. Nobody could overlook a trunk as big as a barn.

Mer. Hadn't you better make sure? ,

Flut. [*To Mer.*] If you'll allow me, I'll attend to it.

Lau. [*Cheerfully.*] You are very kind. [*Turns and resumes talk with Sp.*]

Flut. [*To Mer.*] May I put your hat and shawl down here?

Mer. Oh, you havn't been holding them all this while?

Flut. [*Puts hat, etc., on chair,* L. C., *of small table,* L. *hand.*] It was quite a pleasure, I assure you. [*Exits,* C.]

Lid. Uncle, would you show Mr. Flutterby his room? It's next to yours.

Unc. Is it? I hope he don't snore.

Lid. I hope not, but I don't know.

Unc. No matter, I can stuff the key-hole. [*Exits up-stairs,* R. C.]

Mer. [*To Lida.*] It was so fortunate, Mr. Flutterby came with us. He is so attentive. If it were not for him, half my things would certainly be lost, and myself with them. My husband looks after nothing.

Lau. [*Takes up her hat-box carefully.*] Nobody was ever lost on a railroad, my darling.

Lid. [*Crosses to* R. C.] You do him injustice. See how conscientiously he's holding your hat-box.

Lau. [*Explaining.*] My cartridges are in it.

Mer. [*Screams and runs to him.*] Your cartridges packed in with my hat? The feathers will be ruined!

Lau. It was a good idea of mine, to keep the cartridges safe! I knew Flutterby would take the greatest care of my wife's hat. He held the box on his knees all the time.

Mer. Let me look.

Lau. [*Preventing her gently.*] Excuse me. They might explode, and injure the shape of the hat. I'll unpack them.

Mer. [*To Lid.*] What a man he is!

Lid. Let me show you your room. This way! [*As she is going* L., SP. *perceives her and suddenly exits,* R. 2 D. LID. *opens door,* L., *and starts back.*] Heavens! Mr. De Rigby!

Mer. What's the matter? [*Retreats,* L.]

Lid. [*Controlling herself.*] Oh, nothing! [*Gets round to* R.]

RIGBY *entering from* L.

Rigby. I have the honor to present myself in rather an unfinished state. My toilette is not quite *accomplie*, as the French have it. But as you opened the door, I deemed it my duty to appear. But I see—

Lid. [*Hiding her chagrin and introducing,* R. C.] Mr. Digby de Rigby—Mr. Laurens—Mrs. Laurens.

Rig. Why, Laurens, old boy!

Mer. [*To Lid.*] They're old friends.

Rig. Why, old fellow, come to my arms! [*Embrace tragicomically.* LAU. *rattles hat-box against Rig.'s back, as he clasps him in his arms.*]

Mer. Goodness, my hat!

Rig. [*Rubbing his back.*] Your hat is heavy. I suppose it's the latest thing. Felt, no doubt. I felt it.

Lid. I'm so sorry to disturb you, Mr. De Rigby, but that room was intended for your friends.

Rig. It was Spencer's doing. He put me there.

Lid. [R.] It was a mistake.

Rig. Fortunately I havn't unpacked yet. I'll surrender the position at once.

Lau. [*Crosses to* C.] Extraordinary man. Falls in love, and into trouble, with equal ease. Our acquaintance began by my snatching him from a watery grave. When I brought him out, the *billets-doux* floated from his pockets, like feathers from a pillow.

2

RIGBY *re-enters with his things.*

Rigby.   There, ladies, the coast is clear!

NAP *and* JOHN *enter with large trunk,* C.

Lid. [*Crosses to* L.] In there! [*They take trunk* L. 1 E.]
Lau. [*Crossing to door,* L.] You see, my dear, everything safe.
Mer. I hope my hat is. [*Exits,* L., LAU. *follows.*]
Lid. [*To Rig.*] Will you put your things down, please, and excuse me for a moment or two? [*Aside.*] What shall I do with him? [*Exits,* R. 2 D.]

JOHN *and* NAP *come out and exeunt,* C.

Rig. [*Looks round, baggage in hand.*] Certainly! That's a very pretty woman, Laurens' wife. So is Spencer's. It was a good idea of mine to come down for two weeks, and I can stay longer, if I want to. Where did she mean for me to put my things? [*Looks round, goes to door,* R. 1 E., *and looks in.*] Empty! This must be the place. [*Exits,* R. 1 E.]

SPENCER *enters,* C.

Spencer.   This way, Aunt Cornelia!

MRS. PARTRADGE *enters,* C.

This way! I hope you found the journey pleasant.
Mrs. Partradge. Oh, very. But where's Barbie? '[*Calling.*] Barbie, child, come along!
Barbie. [*Outside.*] Coming, aunt!

BARBIE *enters,* C.

Barbie. Coming! [SP. *goes to* Bar., *whom he takes by the hand.*]
Sp. [C.] Lida will be here in a minute, to give you a sister's welcome. She's rather busy. We have a lot of company.
Bar. That's jolly.
Mrs. P. [R.] Don't say "jolly." You mean that the prospect is agreeable. [*To Sp.*] Our young ladies in Massachusetts are afflicted with the worst form of Anglo-mania. She's got a dreadful assortment of "jolly's" and "awful's," with I don't know how many other English importations.

Bar. [L.] I don't consider them any worse than our own Down-Eastisms. I prefer "jolly" to scrumptious any time o'day.

Mrs. P. "Any time o'day!" That'll do, Miss! [*To Sp.*] Whom have you got with you? Old people? Young people?

Sp. Young married couple—two young gentlemen.

Mrs. P. [*Crosses to* C.] My dear, you must dress at once!

Bar. [*Crosses to* C., *close to Sp.*] Are they awfully jolly? I mean, is the prospect agreeable?

Sp. [R.] Very.

Bar. [*To Mrs. P.*] Then I'll wear a train at dinner. I don't want to be taken for a mere child, at the very first.

Mrs. P. [*Crosses to* C.] You'll never be taken for anything else. Mr. Spencer, she's too tall for her years, so you musn't get a wrong impression from her talk.

Sp. Oh, I won't. [*Going to* R.] Lida set these rooms apart for you. [*Crossing to* R. 1 E.]

Mrs. P. Then come along, dear. [*Pulls open door and starts back.*] Oh! [RIG.'s *arm in shirt-sleeves appears, and draws the door close again.*]

Rigby. [*Within.*] Good gracious!

Bar. [L.] What's the matter, aunt?

Mrs. P. [*To Sp.*] There's a gentleman in there! [*To Bar.*] The person we met in the cars. The Duc de Montebello's salesman. The drummer! [*Crosses to* L.]

Sp. Oho! [*Laughs*] That's not bad. We'll drum him out. [*Laughs.*]

Mrs. P. What are you laughing about?

Sp. You'll see in a moment. [*Goes to door.*] Rigby!

Rigby. [*Inside.*] Yes.

Sp. [*Gets* C.] Here's a surprise for you.

Bar. [*To Mrs. P.*] What can he mean?

Mrs. P. [L.] I think I know.

Bar. I see. He's been imposing on them as somebody he isn't!

Mrs. P. He imposed on us as somebody he wasn't.

RIGBY *enters from* R. 1. D.; BAR. *advances to face him, but* MRS. P. *puts her aside.*

Rigby. Now, old boy— [*Sees Bar.*] The angel! [*Crosses to Sp. and sees Mrs. P.*] The devil!

Sp. [L. C.] Allow me, my friend, Mr. Digby de Rigby, recently arrived from England; de Rigby, Mrs. Partradge, my wife's aunt, her niece, Miss Vaughn, my sister-in-law. [*At the introduction* RIG. *advances to each lady.*]

Rig. Ladies! [*Aside.*] I should like the ground to open and swallow me. [*To Bar.*] I had the happiness of meeting you on the train. You probably don't recall the fact.

Bar. [R. C.] Oh, yes—distinctly.

Rig. [*Pleased.*] Ah!

Mrs. P. Distinctly.

Rig. [*Disconcerted.*] Oh! [*Looks dejected.* MRS. P. *turns away, and converses with Sp. about him.*]

Bar. [*Sweetly.*] I had not forgotten your kind attentions.

Rig. [*Brightening.*] You are very good! Who could possibly foresee our meeting here? I had begun to look upon the incident as one "Gone glimmering in the mist of things that were," as the poets put it. [SP. *explains to Mrs. P.*]

Bar. Then I propose we leave it there and begin anew. [*Gives hand.*]

Rig. How gracefully you help me out of my difficulty! So you are not angry?

Bar. · No. I look on it as a good joke.

Rig. You are amiability itself—as good at heart as you are love—

Bar. No more jokes, now—we are acquainted! [*Goes up* R.]

Rig. [*To Sp.*] Old fellow— [*Close to him.*] the niece is an angel.

Sp. You assured me of that before. Now, make your peace with the aunt. I wish you may find *her* one! [*Goes to* BAR., *who sits in front of the fire-place.*]

Rig. [*To Mrs. P.*] Madam, I am inconsolable. What must you think of me? [SP. *and* BAR. *talk.*]

Mrs. P. I should have preferred, for your sake, we had not met again so soon.

Rig. Don't say that. It affords me the opportunity of explaining the little jest to a lady, whose good opinion I am anxious to gain.

Mrs. P. Mr. Spencer tells me that you frequently indulge in these little jokes. He endeavored to make me understand, if I caught his idea, that no one regarded them from you, as they might from another sort of person.

Rig. Forbear, I beg.

Mrs. P. You admit, I suppose, that there should be a limit to jesting with ladies.

Rig. There should be! For instance, nobody would jest with you, not if he knew you! If I had only remembered your niece's kindness in the past—not this one, but the other; or, in fact, perhaps remembered this one, and recollected that Miss Lida, or rather Mrs. Spencer—Paul's wife in fact; that is, I say, if I had only remembered that she—that is, that you— [*Emphasizes the latter part of his speech by pointing on his fingers and finishes with:*] You understand? [*Drops his glass.*]

Bar. [*To Sp.*] Do help him, poor fellow! He's tangling himself all up.

Sp. [*Crosses to Rig.*] The ladies are more than disposed to forgive you, Digby, I'm sure, so let's change the subject. How did you get into that room?

Rig. I understood from your wife, that I was to go in there.

Sp. There must be some mistake. The room belongs to these ladies.

Rig. I beg a thousand pardons. [*Bows to them.*] Fortunately I've not unpacked. I'll beat a retreat at once. [*Exits, R. 1 E.*]

Sp. All right. [*To Mrs. P.*] Isn't he a good creature after all?

Bar. [R.] I like him. He's awful jol— I mean the prospect is agreeable.

Mrs. P. [*Angrily.*] Ahem! [L.] It does seem as if children always liked story-tellers. He actually represented himself as a travelling salesman.

Sp. Well, aunt, you know you didn't take him for anything of the kind.

Mrs. P. Yes, but what could he have taken us for? I don't like him at all! [*Crosses to C.*]

RIGBY *re-enters, loaded with luggage.*

Rigby. Ladies, the apartments are yours.

Sp. Allow me. [*Conducts* MRS P. *to door; she bows stiffly to* Rig. *and exits,* R. 1 E.]

Bar. Au revoir! [*Bows, exits* R. 1 E.]

Rig. [L.] I say, it was an unfortunate position. The aunt seems to have considerable acidity left.

Sp. [R.] Oh, you know how to correct all that.

Rig. [*Still holding his things.*] I'm afraid not. Everything has gone wrong. In the first place I cram her with that champagne story, then take possession of her room! It's fate—*Kismet,* as the Turks say.

LIDA *enters,* R. 2 D., *wrings her hands at sight of Rig.* SP. *makes a gesture of despair to her, unperceived by Rig.* LIDA *runs off,* C.

Rig. Apropos of fate and predestination, my dear boy, where do I sleep? It seems I'm on the wrong floor.

Sp. The fact is, I forgot where we intend to put you. I'll ask my wife if she remembers.

Rig. [*Crosses to* R.] I havn't succeeded in changing my coat, you know, so if you will be so kind— [LIDA *again looks in and disappears.*]

Sp. Pardon me one moment, Lida wants me. [*Exits,* C.]

Rig. There he runs off. I shall certainly get left. Everybody is dressing for dinner, and I can't get a moment for my exterior.

MIMA *enters,* R. U. E.

Mima. Excuse me. I'm looking for Mr. Spencer.

Rig. [R.] Oh, ah! are you a—are you maid here?

Mim. [L.] Some people say I'm made too much of here.

Rig. Clever! *Soubrette,* as they say on the stage. Now then, Susan—

Mim Jemima, if you please—Mima for short. I'm the farmer's daughter.

Rig. "Only a farmer's daughter?" I hope all the farmers in the neighborhood are similarly blessed.

Mim. [*Looking at his luggage.*] Can I help you in any way?

Rig. You can, if you know which is my room.

Mim. Certainly. I suppose you are Mr. Flutterby?

Rig. No. I'm not Mr. Butterfly. I'm Mr. Digby de Rigby.

Mim. [*Shakes her head.*] No such person. No Mr. Rigby.

Rig. [R.] I beg your pardon, oh! [*Looks at labels on his luggage to see that he is the person that it belongs to.*]

Mim. No room for him here. I guess he's one over.

Rig. [*Struck.*] That's it! I'm *de trop.* [*Crosses to* L.] One over, and one to carry. [*Looks at his baggage.*] But, I say, [C.] show me to any empty room.

Mim. [*Shakes her head.*] All full.

Rig. What? That's why they dislodged me from every position!

Mim. You wait here. I'll think of something. Don't go, mind. I'll take care of you. [*Exits,* C.]

Rig. [*Drops baggage.*] Just my luck! Amiable hostess—pretty guests—lovely angel from the railroad—charming farmer's daughter—two weeks' time on my hands—and I must leave them! I hope there's a train.

BARBIE *and* MRS. PARTRADGE *enter from their room,* MERYL *and* LAURENS *from theirs.*

Barbie. Why, Mr. de Rigby, going?
Laurens. Hallo, Rigby! What's up?
Meryl. [L. C.] You're not going away?
Mrs. Partradge. [R.] No fear of that.
Rig. [C.] Well, you see, the fact is—Spencer—that is—I—

SPENCER *and* LIDA *enter,* C.

Spencer. My dear fellow, was anything ever so unfortunate?
Rig. Never mind. It's my fault. I ought to have written. I regret the inconvenience I have already caused—and, if you will let me have the use of your horses—
Lida. The horses?
Sp. What are you thinking of?
Rig. Of leaving at once. I promise myself the pleasure at another time.
Sp. Nothing of the kind.
Bar. Oh, dear!
Mrs. P. Barbie!
Lau. [L., *crosses to* L. C.] I say, Spencer, can't we divide up our closets between him.
Bar. and Mer. Yes, yes! [BAR. *advancing to* Rig., MRS. P. *pulls her back, and she passes around the table to the* R. C. MRS. P. *remonstrates with her.*]
Sp. It's all arranged. [*To* Rig.] You're to stay with us—only we must beg of you to put up with apartments at the farm-house.
Rig. At the farm-house! [*Aside.*] Where the pretty daughter lives. [*Aloud.*] I'm afraid it's too much trouble.
Sp. Not a bit.

MIMA *enters,* C.

Lid. Here comes Mima. She'll show you the way.
Mima. Are you ready? Only through the grounds!
Bar. He'll want a light.
Lid. It's not far. Remember, dinner at seven. We expect you promptly.
Rig. [*Picks up baggage, going up stage.*] I hear and obey, as the Turks say.
Sp. You're not angry?

Rig.   Not a bit.
Mim.   This way.
Lid. and Mer.   Seven, mind!
Rig.   Till seven, *au revoir*, as the angels say.
Bar.   He's overloaded.   Let's help him.
Mer.   Yes, yes!
Mrs. P.   Barbie!   Barbie!
Mim.   No, no!   I will.

All run to assist Rig., Mrs. P. *advances to check* Bar., *who picks up the gun-case, and threatens her into* R. *corner.*

Rig.   Never!   *En route!*   Forward march!

Mim. *leads the way,* Rig. *following.   Rest form animated tableau of farewell.   Waving of handkerchiefs as* Uncle *enters,* C., *on stairs.*

Uncle.   Hello!   [*To Mim.*]   Did you take his sofa, too?
Bar.   No.   We took his room.

CURTAIN, QUICK.

ACT II.

Same scene as last. Night. After dinner of the same day. Lamp on table, R.

SPENCER *is discovered writing at the table.* BARBIE *enters from her room, R. 1 E.*

Barbie. [L.] Not gone yet?

Spencer. Not yet. I'm glad you came down before I left. A pretty girl always brings a sportsman luck.

Bar. You have to thank auntie for it. She began to preach me a sermon, so I ran off. [*Crosses to* C.]

Sp. What fault does she find?

Bar. Just think! She says I received too much attention this evening.

Sp. Ah!

Bar. And that it isn't proper for a young girl. Now I ask you, who is to receive attention? [*Crossing to bell on pedestal and back.*]

Sp. Who, indeed! [*Rings, rises.*]

JOHN *enters,* R. U. E., *receives letter and exits,* C.

Bar. Old ladies can't, married ladies mustn't, so there's nobody but young girls left—and yet we're scolded.

Sp. What did she say to that admirable presentation of the case?

Bar. You should have heard! But I know it's all her prejudice against poor Mr. De Rigby. Now what did we do? I leave it to you! We sat together at table and laughed and joked, and afterwards we looked over your book of photographs together.

Sp. And afterwards he handed you tea, and sat with you to drink it, and finally you sang and played with him.

Bar. [L., *pauses, then fixedly.*] Do *you* want to begin at me, too?

Sp. Oh! no. I want you to enjoy yourself.

Bar. [*Brightly.*] I did enjoy myself very much. He is so awfully jolly.

Sp. So he is. But see here, Barbie, I don't want to preach like aunt; but being your brother-in-law, and having some responsibility, while you are here, I feel bound to say a few cautious words in reason.

Bar. That's all right. Speak to me in reason and I'll listen in reason.

JACKSON *enters* C., *after a knock.* *He is a farmer and gamekeeper, combined, dressed in semi-hunting costume.* *Carries three guns and puts them in vestibule.*

Jackson. [C.] Good evening, sir.

Sp. Ah, Jackson! Wait a moment, will you?

Bar. No, no, attend to your business first. You and I won't get through in a moment. [*Crosses to* L., *sits on sofa and takes book up.*]

Jack. I've cleaned the guns, sir.

Sp. You think we'll have some sport?

Jack. I'll drive you to Hollar's by daybreak, sir, and give the gentlemen as fine a day as they ever had. I know they're all good shots.

Bar. [*Looking up from her book*] Is Mr. De Rigby a good shot, Jackson?

Jack. Yes, Miss. He makes a deal of fun all the time, but it don't interfere with business.

Bar. [*To herself.*] I cannot understand why they are all so down on him.

Jack. I'll send the dogs on ahead of us, to the swale west of Melford; and if you put Mr. Laurens just beyond the chestnuts, and Mr. De Rigby towards the bushes, they'll all have some of the woodcock. The other gentleman, Mr. Flutterby, he don't mind, I reckon, where he's put. I guess he's no sportsman.

Sp. [*Looks at watch.*] We start at ten, sharp. Moon will be full up then. The others have gone to dress. Have the wagon round on time.

Jack. [*Going up* C.] Yes, sir.

Sp. How is Mr. De Rigby doing at your house? I hope your daughter takes good care of him.

Jack. [*Stopping at door.*] No fear of that, sir. She's devoted to him. [*Exits,* R. 3 E.]

Sp. [*To Bar.*] Did you hear that? Now he is devoting himself to Mima.

Bar. [*Seated,* L.] Jackson didn't say that. He only said *she* was devoted to him. And I can't blame her. He has evidently treated her with the unvarying politeness, which he shows to every woman.

Sp. [*Crossing and sitting beside her.*] Now look here, my dear child—

Bar. [*Warningly.*] We are to talk in reason.

Sp. Certainly. To begin, I know my friend Rigby thoroughly, and I must tell you, that his habit is to flatter all your sex indiscriminately.

Bar. I think it is a very nice habit.

Sp. Certainly. But the ladies must not take it too seriously.

Bar. Ah! I grant you that. But I must say, that he never flatters me the least bit.

Sp. Ah!—now come.

Bar. However, it's just as well you warned me. I'll be very careful. I'll sit next to him at table for the last time to-morrow, and observe him carefully.

Sp. You seem to take a great deal of interest in him.

Bar. How can I help it? First aunt warns me against him, and now you.

Sp. I don't warn you against *him*, but against yourself.

Bar. [*Piqued, rises.*] That is quite unnecessary. [*Crosses to* R.] You needn't think that I can be caught as easily as my sister was. [SP. *looks blank and digs his hands into his pockets.*]

LIDA *enters,* R. 2 D., *with Spencer's small bag and strap in her hand, stops.*

Lida. Well, well! What's the matter here?

Sp. Declaration of Independence by the colony of Massachussetts Bay!

Bar. I'll go back to aunt. She's talked out at least, and I can have some rest. [*Exits,* R. 1 E.]

Lid. I want to ask you about this bag, Paul. Will this do, or will you take the valise, too?

Sp. Why, my darling, from the preparations you make, one would think I was off for a week—when we'll only be gone for a day and back for dinner to-morrow. That's enough. Put everything else in a hamper.

Lid. We'll pack it at once.

Sp. And I can talk to you, meanwhile, about Barbie.

Lid. [R.] About Barbie?

Sp. Yes, you'll have all day to-morrow to attack her.

Lid. Attack her—about what?

Sp. Well, I don't exactly know myself. [*Crosses to* R.] Ask your aunt.

Lid. My dear, don't forget one thing.

Sp. What is that?

Lid.   Barbie and I are sisters.

Sp.   Charming ones.

Lid.   And we never can bear a lecture, except—

Sp.   Why, you always listened to me!

Lid.   I was about to state the exception.   We never take a lecture, except from one we love.   [*Exits,* R. 2 E.]

Sp.   Oh! that never struck me before.   I'm an idiot!   [*Exits after Lid.*]

MIMA *enters,* R. U. E., *passing Sp., and bearing a tray with tea-pot, etc.* JACKSON *following with gun, which he puts against table,* R.

Jackson.   [R.]   Give me another cup.

Mima.   Why, papa! three cups of tea!   No, sir, not another drop!   You'll certainly turn into an old maid.

Jack.   If tea-drinking does that, I wish you'd take to it furiously.

Mim.   [*Puts tray on cabinet,* L.]   Why, papa?

Jack.   There's a deal too much attention paid you, to please me.   I want you for the next ten years—no less.

Mim.   Don't be afraid, papa.   Nobody will carry me off.   When will you be back?

Jack.   [R., *feeling in his pockets.*]   To-morrow night.   Confound it!

Mim.   [*Produces pipe and pouch from her pocket.*]   Looking for your pipe?   Here it is—you forgot and left it on the table.

Jack.   That's my girl!   [*Loading his pipe.*]

Mim.   Mr. De Rigby said it was a jolly old piece of briar wood.   I think he's very nice, don't you, papa?   [*Striking match for him.*]

Jack.   I'll tell you after he's gone.   We musn't judge people too hastily.

Mim.   You have no idea how many pretty things he carries in his valise.   I spread them all out on his table.   The loveliest note-paper, and envelopes, and puff-boxes, and ivory brushes, and bottles of scents—they perfume the whole room.

Jack.   He's just the sort of dandy to catch you gals!   Bah—you havn't a drop of hunter's blood in you!   But if it comes to singing and playing the pianner, or that other new-fangled thing—the sicker—

Mim.   The zither, papa.

Jack.   Or working blue monkeys on a fine screen, you don't take odds from no one.   Such an infernal lot of useless accomplishments for a gal, I never hurd on.

Mim.   [*Defiantly.*]   But that ain't all I can do!   I can cook anything you can give a name to! I can make every stitch I've got on! As for singing, I admit I'm fond of it.

Jack. [R., *dryly.*] Which do you like best—solos or *duetts?*

Mim. [*Falters.*] What do you mean, papa? [*Walks away.*]

Jack. I've been wanting to talk to you for some time. [*Goes up to see if they are alone, then goes to fire-place.*] Come here to me!

Mim. [*Close to the tea-things at cabinet.*] I can hear very well where I am.

Jack. Dodging like a grouse! Well, to speak plainly, I don't like your duetts with that fellow from the drug store.

Mim. [*Who has been nervously fussing with tea-cup.*] Heavens! [*Drops it.*] It slipped from my fingers.

Jack. It slipped from your bad conscience!

Mim. I havn't got a bad conscience—although I do sing with young Mr. Blum in church. Is that wrong?

Jack. Sing with him—no! But I saw him squeeze your hand turning over the music! The infernal, impudent, Dutch apothecary rascal! He's got more assurance than forty Yankees put together!

Mim. [*Amazed.*] Why, papa! he's exceedingly bashful! It's hereditary and is quite a defect. It runs in his family.

Jack. It's run out of his family ever since he was born, then! How a sensible, clean American girl like you can fancy a man, who smells of carbolic soap a mile off—beats me!

Mim. You've just happened to meet him, when he's been mixing.

Jack. Well, I don't like his mixing with you—that's flat! Listen to my first and last say on the subject: No pill-grinder shall have my daughter! [MIM. *throws herself, pouting, into sofa,* L.] Don't cry, now—it's all for your good. [*He goes to her.*] You leave it to me, and I'll get you a nice young fellow from the neighborhood.

Mim. [*Sobs.*] I don't want a nice young fellow from the neighborhood!

Jack. [*Going to fire to light his pipe, which had gone out.*] Of course not! domestic goods never take with the women! It's the imported article they want! [*Ring at the bell,* C. D.]

Mim. Goodness! [*Runs to door, opens it, and sees Blum, shuts it quickly, holding it close.*]

Jack. Who is it?

Mim. I—oh—oh!

Blum. [*Outside.*] Good evening, Miss Mima!

Jack. It's the Dutchman! He's just in time to get a piece of my mind!

Mim. Papa, I beg of you not to be rude! Remember, we are not in our own house, and Mr. Blum don't come here to see us. And, anyway, a person of his retiring disposition is easily hurt. [BLUM *tries to rush in the door, she keeps her back to it.*] If he were a forward, pushing character—

BLUM bursts in.

Mim. Oh!

Blum. [*Backs on, bumping the door open.*] Aha! I got him open! He sticks! [*Examines door and tries it.*] What he sticks for? [*Sees Mim.*] Oh, it was you sticks him? It was fun—you was making some jokes?

Mim. [L.] Don't you see papa?

Bl. [*Going to Jack., stepping over gun.*] Ah, papa! Lieber papa! good evening! [*Tries to take Jack.'s hand, and insists, at last, on shaking it.*] Aha! You makes some jokes, too! You shall shake me! you got noding de matter with your hand dere! [*Surveys him.*] And how you was des time? You was well looking—you was looking good. Ha! ha! you don't want some drug stores!

Jack. [R.] No—nor no druggists neither!

Bl. Ha! ha! ha! Tat was goot! I tell dat everywhere. Den everybody laughs at you.

Jack. [*Curtly.*] Do you want to see me?

Bl. [C.] Yes. I was at your house, and dey say you was up here. You know dat Mr. Groobie—my boss, what you call it. Well, he was, what dey say—he was going out cunning to-morrow.

Jack. Cunning to-morrow?

Bl. Chooding. To knock over some birds. Dis way— [*Takes up gun and points at Jack.*]

Jack. Put that thing down. You mean he's going shooting, I understand. [*Aside.*] Infernal monkey!

Bl. I thought I makes you understand.

Jack. Well, what does Mr. Groobie want?

Bl. Well, Mr. Groobie he is got a cun, but he is got no gardriges. He say you know his cun—it was a bridge-loader like Mr. Spencer, and he wants some cardriges, if you got some more dan dere is birds to choot.

Jack. I'll give him some in a second. Just wait here. [*Going,* C.]

Bl. I guess he don't want some with too much powder, dot blows him backwards.

Jack. I make my cartridges right. He can depend upon that. [*At door,* C., *gives a warning look to Mim., and exits,* C.]

Bl. [*Seizing Mim. around the waist and bringing her down.*] Shust imagine how I was dat delighted when Mr. Groobie he found he was out of gardriges and I had to come.

Mim. [L.] It was our lucky star.

Bl. Yes, I was dot star. I dook gare to drop dose gardriges down de well myself.

Mim. Good gracious!

Bl. It makes noding. It was healthy for the water, and I ran here all de way—over de stones and through the dark.

Mim. How did you get on without falling?

Bl. I didn't. I just come on my hands and knees all the way.

Mim. Are you sure you're not hurt?

Bl. It is noding. What hurts me is dat your fader, he is not lovely to me.

Mim. No, indeed. It was just before you came in, he said—

Bl. What?

Mim. Hush! Here he is.

Bl. But my darling. [*Sings*] " *Tra-la-la!*"

She darts away, as JACKSON *re-enters.*

Jackson. Did you speak to me?

Bl. It is noding. I was making a little sing-song mit my troat.

Jack. It sounded very affectionate. Here are the cartridges.

Bl. How much dey is? [*Hand in pocket.*]

Jack. [*Crosses to* R.] Oh, I'll see him myself. Tell him the party starts at ten.

Bl. Den I'll be off.

Jack. You havn't got a moment to lose.

Bl. [*Takes Jack.'s reluctant hand.*] Good night. I hope you have luck.

Jack. [R., *dashing his hand away.*] Go to the devil!

Mim. [R. C.] Now you have done it.

Bl. [C.] What haft I done?

Jack. Don't you know, you stick of liquorice, that you never ought to wish a man luck in shooting? It spoils the whole day. [MIM. *nods to Blum in confirmation as he turns to her.*]

Bl. So? I beg ten thousand pardons. But I make it all right. I hope I may die den, if I don't wish dat you never hit a bird and dat you choot one anoder. [*Exits precipitately,* C.]

Jack. [*Threatens with gun.*] Get out! [*Steps towards door,* C.] That's a pretty fellow for a husband! Deuced ignorance, combined with the cheek of the devil.

Mim.   You can't expect a doctor to know much about shooting.
Jack.   No, he does his killing another way.
Mim.   Oh, papa!
Jack.   You're a good girl, and worthy a better husband than a poison mixer. Reflect on what I've said. [*Exits,* R. U. E.]
Mim.   Yes, papa, I'll reflect. [*Goes to window,* L. C.]   The only way to get around father is to pretend to give in. And I must get around him—for it's no use, I cannot give up my Theobald.

[*Song in which* BLUM *joins, opening the window and looking in.*]

> Love is everywhere;
>   From its pains who is ever free?
> And its bondage, so lovers declare,
>   Far sweeter is than liberty !
> While the moonlight is beaming so fair,
> And night birds sweetly singing.
>   To deny Love's dominion
>   What mortal can dare?
> A maiden finds Love everywhere.
>   To deny Love's dominion
>   What mortal can dare?
>   A maiden finds Love everywhere.

Mim.   You havn't gone?
Blum.   [*At window.*]   I couldn't until you told me what your fader said.
Mim.   He has forbidden me to have anything to do with you.
Blum.   Den we must bart forever.
Mim.   We must. [*Goes down stage.*]

BLUM *looks after her, then leaves window and comes in, steals down, putting his arm around her waist.*

Blum.   Chemima! Let us talk over dat parting.
Mim.   [L.]   Don't!
Bl.   [R.]   Will anybody come?
Mim.   No. They are all in their rooms or busy. The gentlemen are getting ready to start for the game to-night,
Bl.   [*Puts bag of cartridges on table,* R.]   And your fader—where is he gone?
Mim.   To the cottage for the wagon. He won't be back for some time.
Bl.   Suppose he forgot something, and come back right away quick?
Mim.   What have we to be afraid of? You can explain to him.

Bl. Yes, if he gif me some time. He is pretty quick, you know.

Mim. [*Musingly.*] It might precipitate matters.

Bl. So it might, unless I run.

Mim. I mean, it would compel us to declare our feelings. Oh, how he does hate foreigners! He says he don't know how I can love a Dutchman!

Bl. Don't he! Vell, just let him fall in love with a German girl once! He gets so grazy, he don't know nodings. [*Buttons his coat.*] De next time I meet him I brobose. I don't was afraid of him. A fader don't haf no right to keep from his daughter de berson what she loffs.

Mim. Don't begin by rousing his wrath.

Bl. He has roused my rats. I stand no nonsense.

Flutterby. [*Outside.*] I tell you it's all right, my dear fellow.

Mim. Hush! Oh, that's him!

Bl. [*Wilting.*] I guess I better not see him just now.

Mim. It's not father—it's Mr. De Rigby.

Bl. [*Jealous.*] Mr.—who?

Mim. One of the guests. He's stopping at the cottage. He's been down there since dinner, getting ready for the hunt.

Bl. Mima—you don't—

Mim. Mr. Flutterby's with him. Don't meet them. Wait till they go away.

Bl. [*Crosses* L. *up.*] I wait outside the door.

Mim. Do—no—they're just at the door. Go in the closet. [*Pulls him round and hurries him into closet under the stair* C.] Don't break anything.

Bl. I smodder in dere.

Mim. You must squeeze in. [*Shutting him in.*] Just in time.

Bl. [*Putting his head out.*] Chemima, which shelf is the brandy peaches on? [*She slams door upon him.*]

RIGBY *and* FLUTTERBY *enter,* C., *in hunting costume.*

Rigby. [C.] Nobody down yet. [*Sees Mim.,* R.] Ah, my young hostess! [*To Flut.*] You have seen my wigwam; let me present the fair squaw, who graces it with her presence. [*Crosses* R. *and sits at table.* MIM. *curtsies.*]

Flutterby. Charming. She even curtsies. Quite an early English squaw. [*Crosses* R.]

Mim. [*Going up,* C.] I wonder how long they'll keep Theobald in the closet?

Rig. Pretty creature, eh?

3

Flut. I don't much care for these children of nature. If you move among women of society, you soon lose your taste for the uncultivated variety.

Rig. The wild strawberry has a flavor of its own, very much to my liking.

Flut. Tastes differ.

Rig. Yes. Have a. cigar? [*Offers case.*]

Flut. Thank you, I prefer cigarettes, [*Takes out small case.* Rig. *lights his cigar.* Flut. *watches him without lighting his.*] They say he makes love to every woman he meets. He paid Mrs. Laurens marked attention this evening. I'll find out his game, and what I have to fear in him. [*Spoken aside.*]

Rig. Got a light? [*Offers box.*]

Flut. Thanks. [*Lights cigarette.*]

Mim. [*At back.*] They are going to settle down. Oh dear! [Bl. *puts his head out and quickly withdraws it.*]

Flut. [*Sits.*] You had an enviable seat at dinner.

Rig. Between Mrs. Laurens and Miss Barbie. I was set like a pearl in diamonds.

Flut. I had to do the amiable to the aunt.

Rig. Nice old lady. When I speak to her niece, her eyes become gimlets, and screw into my very soul. I tried to engage her in conversation during one of your frequent pauses. I said, " I hope we shall have a fine day to-morrow."

Flut. Well, how did she take it?

Rig. She told me, I might as well have added that brilliant remark to all the rest I had bestowed on her niece.

Flut. Not bad that.

Rig. No, and done like a flash. It quite stunned me.

Flut. We agree upon the aunt—so pass her over.

Rig. Oh, I pass.

Flut. Which of the others do you like best?

Rig. That's hard to say.

Flut. A connaisseur like you, must have an opinion. You paid them all marked attention.

Rig. [*Flattered.*] You noticed it? That's one of my points. The poetry of my nature, for want of the literary faculty, expresses itself in general homage to the sex.

Flut. Very neatly termed—considering your want of the literary faculty. [*Aside.*] Conceited ass. [*Crash heard in closet.*]

Mim. [*Aside.*] Heavens! he has stepped on something.

Rig. What's that?

Mim. [*Running down* L., *then up.*] That? It must have been the cat.

Rig. Sounded like two or three cats.

Mim. [*Aside.*] Oh, dear! [*Aloud.*] Puss! puss! puss! [*Exits*, R. U. E.]

Flut. [*Crosses to* L.] I see that you are too much of a diplomat, to show your hand. But, as we are the only bachelors in the house, suppose we confide in each other—just enough to avoid competition.

Rig. [R.] Very sensible idea.

Flut. [*Offers hand.*] We will hold nothing back.

Rig. [*Takes hand.*] Make a clean breast of it. You begin.

Flut. I'm quite willing. [*Suddenly.*] What do you think of Mrs. Laurens?

Rig. Mrs. Laurens? Charming! Harmony in face, form, voice, mind, dress and everything—a poem! a rhythm of nature, metaphysically speaking.

Flut. [*Aside.*] I suspected it. But I'll save her.

Rig. You are silent. You don't agree with me?

Flut. On the contrary—it's precisely my idea of her.

Rig. [*Sighs.*] But she's married.

Flut. You find that embarrassing?

Rig. Naturally. She's an appropriated treasure. Laurens is a happy man. So is she. I mean they are a happy couple.

Flut. It *is* an obstacle.

Rig. It's an obstacle there's no getting over.

Flut. [R.] Perhaps. [*Sending a curl of smoke out of his mouth.*] Did you ever speculate in stocks?

Rig. No, but another fellow did for me, though! I wish he hadn't.

Flut. Well, sometimes your fancy is at a premium—sometimes it goes down to nothing. That's the way with matrimonial felicity. If you think of investing your attentions profitably, watch the market.

Rig. [*Eye-glass up*, L.] Investing your attentions! That's something new.

Flut. For instance. Last summer I went to Newfoundland with them. Laurens was out all day, hunting white porpoises.

Rig. White porpoises?

Flut. White porpoises.

Rig. Oh, I know, those fellows that turn sommersaults in the air.

Flut. His wife sat for hours on the shore, watching for his return. Stocks were up. No time to buy.

Rig. [R.] You mean the grapes were sour. That's an equally suitable metaphor.

Flut. I waited for a change in the market.

Rig. Indeed! [*Aside.*] The fellow's a dangerous character.

Flut. [*Aside.*] He takes it coolly. The man's a practiced libertine. It's lucky I'm with 'em. [*Loud.*] I think now, that stocks are going down. I predict a crash in the immediate future. [*Crosses to* R., *takes lamp off and goes to staircase.*] Will you go to my room, till they are ready to start?

Rig. No, thank you.

Flut. Excuse the lamp. [*Aside.*] He shan't have ten words with her, while he stays in the house. I'll see to that. [*Goes up with lamp and exits at back up stairs. Stage darkened.*]

Rig. I wish that young gentleman hadn't confided his diabolical plans to me. I feel quite uncomfortable.

MIMA *enters,* R. U. E.

Mima. Are you going to the farm-house, sir?

Rig. No, I think I should prefer staying here for a chat with you.

Mim. Oh, I havn't the time. I have to look after so much, and the wagon will be here presently. Why, you're all in the dark. Shall I get you a lamp?

Rig. No. I'll go and look for the comet. I shall dream of white porpoises for a week. [*Exits,* C.]

BLUM *emerges.*

Blum. Gott im Himmel!

Mim. [*Retreating.*] What a noise you made.

Bl. Don't go, Chemima.

Mim. I must. He's coming back. [*Exits,* R. U. E.]

BLUM *runs back, but puts his head out again; hearing no one, he comes out.*

Blum. Mima! Mima! That's a nice idea! If I can find my ways to the door—[*Stumbles over stairs.*] Where de deuce I leave those gardriges? [*Gropes for them.*]

RIGBY *re-enters,* C.

Rigby. Cigar's gone out. I left my matches here. [*Feels on table and catches Bl.'s hand. Pull to and fro across table.*] Who's this?

Bl. [*Aside, and sinking under table, trying to pull his hand away.*] Jiminy Cripps! was dot her fader?

Rig. Speak, can't you? Who the dickens have I got hold of?

Bl. If you will be so kind and let go my hand.

Rig. Strange voice! What do you want here? [*Seizes him by the collar.*] What are you crawling about for?

MIMA *re-enters with lamp, shading it with her hand. Stage lightened.*

Mima. He must have got away by this time. [*Sees the group.*] Oh! [*Gives a little scream.*]

Bl. Please, Miss Cheminia, tell him it was all right.

Rig. [*Looks at both and releases him.*] I see. It's the cat. I beg a thousand pardons. Don't let me interrupt the feline concert. [*About to go.*]

Mim. [*Places lamp on table, up stage, and intercepts him.*] No, you shan't go away like that.

Rig. [C.] But, my dear—

Mim. [L., *in tears and indignant.*] You must listen to me. We love one another.

Rig. Accept my congratulations—but, as a third party is superfluous in such cases—

Mim. It's not a laughing matter.

Bl. No, it wasn't. It's no choke. We are met for de last time. Her fader won't haf me.

Rig. It's growing tragical.

Mim. We first saw each other at the singing school.

Rig. Getting musical. Just the place to establish harmonious relations.

Mim. [*Introducing.*] Mr. de Rigby—Mr. Blum.

Rig. How do you do, Mr. Blum. I regret that our first acquaintance was made in the dark.

Bl. Dot's right. I have to keep in de dark as much as possible. Her fader won't haf no druggist. It's a good business, too.

Rig. Very, for the proprietor. [*Takes a hand of each.*] Well, my children, and so you are wretched?

Mim. Yes.

Rig. Be comforted. Think of Abelard and Heloise.

Bl. Was you acquainted with them?

Rig. Not personally. But then, remember that poison party, Romeo and Juliet, and that water party, Hero and Leander!

Bl. [R.] That's so, Mima. If your fader separates us, we drown ourself, or we poison de lemonade.

Rig. Let us look the matter calmly in the face. We have one thing on our side. You love each other.

Bl. and Mim. We do.

Rig. [c.] I've been in love myself.

Mim. [L.] I'm so glad! [*Both take his hands.*]

Bl. You know how it was yourself.

Rig. And I have learnt one lesson. If a woman loves a man she will have him.

Mim. Then *she* didn't love *you!*

Rig. Evidently. But, as you love him, we will succeed. I will be your friend, and, as the story book says, all will be well. [*Crosses to* L. *Noise of wagon and whips outside.*]

Mim. Hark! There's father and the dogs. [*To Bl.*] Run! No, wait. I'll go with you. The dogs mightn't know you, and if they saw you running—

Bl. I mightn't like it, neither.

Mim. Come with me. It's all right. [*Runs back.*] Thank you, Mr. de Rigby, from the bottom of my heart.

Bl. [*Runs back.*] I dank you, doo! [*Embraces him and is pulled back by* MIM., c.]

Rig. [*Lights cigar.*] This is too touching, and if it wasn't for the white porpoises that keep continually leaping up in my head, I could enjoy the situation. Confound that young scamp and his quotations in the matrimonial market. [*Exits*, c.]

Noise of whips. BARBIE *runs in from her room,* R. 1 E.

Barbie. What's all the noise about, I wonder.

SPENCER *entering from* R. U. E., *in shooting dress, with* LIDA.

Spencer. It's the dogs. Jackson has just arrived with them in the wagon.

Lida. [c.] At what hour shall we have dinner to-morrow, dear?

Sp. [L.] It's very uncertain, darling, when we shall get back. It all depends upon the woodcock.

Lid. Well, about what hour, do you think?

Sp. Anywhere between six and nine.

Lid. Three hours! Everything will be spoiled.

Sp. We shan't mind if we have a good day.

Bar. [*Coming down* R.] You won't mind. But what are we to do? [*To Lid.*] That just shows what men are! But it's the fault of the wives—they don't manage right.

Lid. Indeed! What would you call proper management in a case like this?

Bar. [*Firmly, crosses to* c.] I would say : My darling, we dine at six, so arrange to be punctual.

Sp. [*To Lid.,* L.] There, my dear.

Bar. [c.] My heart bleeds for you, Lida, when I see how you submit to your tyrant.

Lid. [R.] But Paul is not a tyrant.

Bar. Yes he is, and so are all the men, and yet they can be twisted around a woman's little finger.

Lid. I thought so once. Get married, and you'll find out the mistake.

Bar. I'll take precious good care not to. But I'll prove I'm right, all the same. I shall command, and I shall be obeyed! [*Crosses to* L., *she lays on sofa, her head resting on two cushions.*]

Lid. You're a little goose.

LAURENS *in shooting dress and* MERYL *enter from their room,* L.

Meryl. [*Crossing to* c.] What do you think I've been doing ever since dinner—making cartridges.

Laurens. [*Patting her cheek.*] You couldn't spend your time better. [BAR. *shrugs her shoulders, and curls herself on sofa with a book,* L.]

Mer. But the worst of it was, I had to listen all the time to accounts of my liege lord's wonderful shots.

Lau. Instructive, as well as amusing. [*To Sp.*] Did I ever tell you about that remarkable shot—

Mer. [*To Lau.*] There, there! that'll do. Spare me any more of it. [*Brings him down front.*] Did you remember, dear, that to-morrow was mother's birthday?

Lau. Is it? I quite forgot.

Mer. I hope you'll write to her.

Lau. Yes, I'll send her a telegram to-night.

Mer. No, no, telegrams always alarm her. You can just add a line to my letter. It won't take a moment. Do it now. [*Urging him off.*]

Lau. I will, just as soon as I've seen the dogs safe in the cart. Pont never stops howling till he sees me.

Sp. I'll go with you. [*Exeunt,* c.]

Lid. Men's solicitude for dogs is something touching.

Mer. It's a sad thing for us. Take my advice, and never let your husband become so infatuated with sport.

Lid. Oh, let them enjoy themselves. It makes them good tempered.

Mer. What's the use of their good tempers, if they are never home? That's the trouble with the sporting fever. It depopu-

lates the fireside, and it's all the worse because it's apparently so
innocent.   The man who gambles or drinks, is open to reproach,
but a man fond of yachting, or fishing, or shooting—it's so harmless!   But it enables them to get away from us, and stay away
all the same, I notice.

Bar.   [*Pretending to read, now looks over her book.*]   This is
very instructive.   No fishing or shooting when I get married!

Lid.   [*To Mer.*]   You exaggerate.   [*Laughs.*]

Mer.   Oh, there was a time, when I laughed too.   We made
our tour of Europe in the dog days, so that Laurens could be
back in time for the woodcock.   Now I don't laugh.   I know
that his dog and gun are dearer than his wife.

Lid.   Oh, oh!   [*Crosses to* c.]

Bar.   [*Aside.*]   I think myself that's rather strong.

Lid.   My husband can never get to that point.

Mer.   [R.]   I sincerely hope that you are not cherishing
illusions.

Bar.   [*Aloud.*]   And so do I.

Lid.   You shall see.   I mean to ask him in your presence
whether he prefers sport to his home.

Bar.   How green you are!   [*Jumping up.*]   Of course he'll
say just what you wish, and go on and *do* exactly as he pleases.

Lid.   No, he will not.   It's a question of honor with me
now to justify him, and I'll do it.   I'll ask him to remain at
home to-morrow.   He will remain.   That will be proof sufficient,
I imagine.

Mer.   It will be a great deal, certainly.

Lid.   [*To Bar.*]   Don't you tell him what I want him to do.
Don't say a word.   [*Crosses to* R.]

Bar.   I won't.   I'm here to learn, and the prospect looks very
agreeable.   [*Sits on sofa,* L.]

Mer.   Well, I'll assist you with an experiment on my husband.
I'll ask him so stay home to-morrow.   I wish I may get it.

Lid.   If we unite our forces, success is certain.

MRS. PARTRADGE *enters,* R. 1 E.

Mrs. Partradge.   Where's Barbie?

Lid.   You're just in time, aunt.   We need you for a conspiracy.   [*Crosses to her.*]

Mrs. P.   [*Crosses to* R. C.]   A conspiracy?

Lid.   Against our husbands.

Mrs. P.   [*Crosses to* L. C.]   I'm with you.   Anything against
the men.

Lid.   They are to be forced to give up their day's shooting,
and stay with us.

Mrs. P. Well, and what am I to do?

Lid. [*Crosses to* R. C.] We are to make the first assault, and, in case of repulse, you are to come up.

Bar. You are to act as heavy artillery, auntie.

Mrs. P. And what are you to be, Miss?

Bar. I'm to take up my position as a corps of observation—look on and learn ever so much.

Mrs. P. That'll be a very good thing for you—if you can do it.

Mer. Hsh! Here they come.

FLUTTERBY *enters from staircase, in fancy hunting suit.*
LAURENS *and* SPENCER, C.

Spencer. Anybody seen Rigby? He'll be late.

Flutterby. [*Looking at Mer.*] He'll be along presently. Detained, no doubt, making pretty speeches to his hostess. He appears to be much smitten with the wild strawberry.

Bar. [*Aside, angrily on sofa,* L.] Now what a gratuitous piece of idiocy that is! Now I hate that man!

Flut. [*Tenderly to Mer.*] You look as if something disturbed you. Not ill, I hope?

Mer. [*Loud and breaking from Flut.*] You are ready to start, I see.

Flut. Yes. Precious bore! One has hardly time to say a word, before these Nimrods hurry him off. [MER. *goes to Lau.,* FLUT. *to Mrs. P.,* SP. *and* LID. *come down.*]

Lid. I have a great favor to ask of you, Paul.

Sp. [*Tenderly.*] What is it, darling?

Lid. Give up shooting to-morrow, and stay with us.

Sp. [*Both come down,* C.] Hey! How you frightened me—I thought you were in earnest. You're joking!

Lid. No, I'm not. You can't tell how much I value this! You will do as I ask—won't you?

Sp. [*Looks at Lau., to whom* MER. *is eagerly talking.*] But what will Laurens say? I invited him here expressly to—

Lid. [*Both get toward* R.] We will amuse him. He will stay, if you do. [LAU. *comes down, laughing, followed by* MER., *who is very serious.*]

Sp. [*To Lau.*] Well, what do you say?

Lau. [L., *to Sp.*] Stay at home in such weather! It's nonsense! Impossible! [MER. *pulls him back and talks to him.*]

Sp. [*To Lid.*] Did you hear that?

Lid. If you remain, none of the others will go. Do grant me this favor.

Sp. But why? Only tell me why?

Lid. The reason don't matter. I beg you—that ought to be enough!

Sp. I must say, all this appears very childish. [*Turns away up* R., *she follows him.*]

Lid. But Paul—

Bar. [*On her sofa.*] It's getting serious. [MRS. P. *comes down and sits by Bar.* MER. *comes down,* R., *with* LAU.]

Mer. I ask it, as a proof of your affection for me.

Lau. I can show my affection in a more sensible manner. It would be folly, to yield to a mere caprice. I say, Spencer, you wouldn't allow yourself to be coaxed, would you?

Sp. [*After a glance at Lid.*] Certainly not. We start at once!

Lau. That's sensible.

Lid. [*Sinks on chair.*] I'm an unhappy woman!

Mer. [*Goes to Lid.*] I pity you from my heart.

Bar. [*Aside to Mrs. P.*] Now, auntie, your turn. Bring up your heavy artillery!

Mrs. P. [*Rising majestically.*] Gentlemen! [LAU. *and* SP. *turn respectfully.*] If you knew the awful dream I had last night, you would stay at home, as your wives request. [SP. *and* LAU. *look at each other and wink.*] I dreamt that I saw you [*To Lau.*] lying on the ground, dangerously wounded.

Mer. Oh! [*Shrieks and covers her face.*]

Lau. Saw me?

Mrs. P. Yes—stretched upon the earth and covered with blood!

Lau. Capital! [*Runs to her and shakes her hand heartily.*] It's immensely lucky. We shall have a splendid day. You couldn't have had a better dream! [BAR. *gives her a look of triumph and exultation, and shakes both her hands mockingly.* MRS. P. *sinks on sofa.*]

Bar. Artillery utterly defeated.

Sp. Lida, be sensible. Dreams are all stuff.

Lid. Let me be! [*Sobbing.*]

Mer. [*To Lau.*] Pause! It is a question of life and death!

Lau. Yes—for the birds. [*Kisses her.*]

Mer. Go away! [*Sobs and wipes kisses off.*]

RIGBY *enters from* C., *with gun and game-bag, cheerily; leaves gun in vestibule.*

Rigby. [*Up* C.] Well, are we ready for the start?

Sp. and Lau. Yes, all ready. [*They go up and get bags, gun, etc.*]

Rig. [*Glass up, eyes Lid. and Mer.*] What's the matter here, I wonder?

Bar. [*Aside, rising.*] The others tried their persuasions and failed. Now I'll see, what I can do. [*Crosses to* C. LAU. *takes his overcoat from the rack, and puts it on.*]

Mrs. P. [*To Bar., stopping her.*] Where are you going?

Bar. I'm going—

Mrs. P. Where?

Bar. To make an attack in another quarter. Good evening, Mr. De Rigby!

Rig. Ah, here's one bright face at last!

Bar. Mr. De Rigby, you are a devoted sportsman, are you not?

Rig. Certainly.

Bar. You are infatuated—wrapped up heart and soul in it?

Rig. Heart and soul and the rest of the structure.

Bar. Now, suppose I were to ask you to stay at home to-morrow—would you do it?

Rig. [*Adjusts glasses and looks at her.*] I don't quite catch.

Bar. I suppose you are thinking over the politest form of refusal.

Mrs. P. [*Going to Bar.*] Barbie! [*Crosses to Rig.*] Go shooting, Mr. De Rigby, the others are waiting for you.

Bar. You can go if you like, of course. [*Stage* L.]

Rig. Miss Barbie, to borrow the expression of a famous states-man: "Here I am—here I stay." [*Takes off game-bag.*] Allow me to disarm. [*Goes up and puts away bag, etc.* BAR. *looks triumphantly at Mrs. P., and tries to take her hands.*]

Mrs. P. [*Very angry.*] Barbie, this is scandalous! How dare you act in this manner?

Bar. [*Back to sofa.*] It's only a joke.

Mrs. P. A pretty joke! What will he think?

Bar. Probably, that I want him to play croquet with me. Look how the other two hang their heads!

Sp. [*To Rig.*] Are you really not going?

Rig. No. I remain with the ladies.

Flut. [*Eyes Rig. and Mer. jealously.*] With your permission, I will remain too. [*To Sp.*]

Sp. Just as you please.

Lau. Let the slaves stay. We, at least, are free.

NAP *enters,* C.

Nap. Wagon's ready, sir!

Sp. I say, Laurens, let's give it up.

Lau. Nonsense!

Sp. [*To Nap.*] Nap, if Mr. Groobie comes, you bring him along after us. *En avant!* Good night, ladies, till to-morrow. [SP. and LAU. *turn back to kiss their wives, who are sulking, then they exeunt.* NAP. *after them.*]

Rig. [*To Flut., coming down.*] Do you know what's the matter? [*The ladies are all up stage.*]

Flut. There was a scene between Laurens and his wife.

Rig. Ah! I see.

Flut. A sort of panic in the market.

Rig. [*Aside.*] There he goes with the white porpoises again. Deuce take the fellow! [*Crosses to* L.]

Flut. Prices down. Now is the time to try one's luck. I'll console her for his absence. You entertain the others. Get them out of the way. [*Goes up to Mer.*]

Rig. [*Aside.*] Get them out of the way? Confound his impudence. I'll see that you don't have things *all* your way.

Bar. [*Rises, goes to window.*] There's a lovely moon. Wouldn't it be awfully jolly to walk down the road, and see them start. [*Turns up stage, speaks joyfully to her aunt as she passes.*] We're going down the road to see them start.

Rig. I'm at your orders, Miss Barbie.

Flut. [*To Mer.*] Won't you go?

Mer. No, thank you.

Rig. [*Getting shawl, etc.*] Are you coming, Flutterby?

Flut. No, I think I shall stay here.

Bar. Oh, yes, do come, Mr. Flutterby.

Rig. [*Brings shawl, etc., down, and loads Flut.*] Miss Barbie insists on your looking at the moon.

Flut. [*Aside.*] Confound it! [*Aloud.*] Oh, if Miss Barbie insists—

Bar. Certainly. Come along, Mr. De Rigby. [*Exits,* C.] [RIG. *exits after, dragging* FLUT.]

Mrs. P. Arn't either of you going?

Lid. [*Down* R. C.] No.

Mrs. P. Somebody must go with that girl. Dear, dear, and I've got my thin shoes on.

Lid. I can't help it. I've got a headache. I can't go out. [*Crosses to sofa.*]

Mer. [R.] Please excuse me.

Mrs. P. She must not be left to herself. If I can find a pair of rubbers—that grass is like a pond, I know. [*Gets a pair at back.*] What on earth girls can see in the moon, I don't know —unless it be the man in it. [*Exits,* C.]

Mer. [*Coming to Lid.*] I'm so sorry I got you into this scrape.

Lid. I am thoroughly unhappy, for the first time.

Mer. As the older married woman, I ought not to have per-mitted the experiment.

Lid. It is better as it is. I know now, what I have to depend upon. [*Rises, crosses to* R.]

Mer. Don't take it too much to heart. Put yourself in his place. Suppose you were dressed for a ball, and, just as you were stepping into the carriage, he asked you, without giving any rea-son, to stay at home. Would you have complied? No!

Lid. That would be a foolish request—without giving a suf-ficient reason. And yet if he had begged me, as I have begged him—

Mer. [*Interrupting.*] You would have shed a few tears—and gone after all.

Lid. He went without any tears. [*Crosses to* L.]

Mer. And at this moment he feels miserable.

Lid. Do you think so? That would be some consolation.

Mer. It's nothing to what they deserve. They must be pun-ished.

Lid. Punished?

Mer. I won't rest until I make my gentleman feel as mortified as I do. [*Crosses to* L.]

UNCLE JOYCE *enters*, L. U. E.

Uncle. [C.] Well, my dears—your truants have run off, eh? There—there—don't look so blue.

Lid. [R.] Uncle, what is the surest way to make a man un-comfortable?

Unc. What?

Lid. Not a little uncomfortable—but almost quite thoroughly wretched.

Unc. Take away his sofa.

Lid. I'm serious.

Unc. So am I.

Lid. Now you must be good. Tell us how to get even with these lords of creation, who desert us in such a cavalier fashion.

Unc. They leave you moping at home. Treat them in just the opposite way. Celebrate their return with a ball—a house full of company.

Lid. [*To Mer., joyous.*] The very thing.

Mer. [*To. Lid.*] An inspiration! If there is one thing these outdoor fellows abominate more than another, it's dancing.

Lid. Just the way with my despot. I have to send regrets to half the receptions. Now I'll give a ball myself.

Unc. Good! I'll just pack up a few things, and slip away to-night, till it's over.

Lid. and Mer. [*Both seize him.*] Uncle! Uncle! [*As they turn him around.*]

Lid. No. We want you. You must give me the names of everybody in the neighborhood we ought to invite, and you must get us the music, and all the young men you can. [*He is going.*]

Mer. [*Pulls him back.*] Lida! Another inspiration!

Lid. What is it? [*Holding Uncle.*]

Mer. Mr. De Rigby—

Lid. What about him?

Mer. [L.] I'll confide to my husband, as a fatal secret, that Mr. De Rigby is paying you the most marked attention.

Lid. Yes— [*Laughs.*]

Mer. At the same time, you give your husband the same information, in the strictest confidence, about Mr. De Rigby and me.

Lid. What will they do?

Mer. They'll give up shooting for the whole season—stay at home, to watch us and protect each other. We will flirt madly with the object of suspicion, while our lords and masters undergo grinding torments.

Unc. [*Sinks in chair, crosses to* R.] But will De Rigby act this part?

Mer. [*Crosses to him.*] Act? No need to ask him! It's his nature. He can't help himself—we begin to-morrow.

Lid. [*Going up towards* R. U. E.] To-morrow!

Unc. Go on, children, go on! This beats the sofa trick.

QUICK CURTAIN.

ACT III.

Same as last: Evening again. JOHN *discovered lighting the candelabras about.* SUSAN *arranging the flower-stands in the window.* MIMA *enters from* L. U. E., *and* NAP, *with a tray of bon-bons,* R. U. E.

Mima. Everything looks lovely, John; you can light up the parlors, it's most time for the company to come. Susan, you go and look your best, in case you're needed. [JOHN *and* SUSAN *exeunt,* R. U. E.]

Nap. [L.] Whar'll I put these, Miss Mima?

Mim. There, on the sideboard, Nap—they won't be wanted until the dancing begins.

Nap. Mus' I hand 'em round, then?

Mim. No, not till I tell you. When the æsthetic cotillion begins, then you're to let each lady and gentleman select one.

Nap. Den dey pull and pop 'em, eh?

Mim. Yes, there; go along. I'll tell you, when to pass them round. [NAP *exits,* R. U. E.]

RIGBY *entering,* C.

Rigby. Ah, the wild strawberry is first in the field! The ladies have not come forth yet?

Mim. [R.] No, they're still dressing for the ball.

Rig. [L.] Then I may as well be patient for a couple of hours. Ah! [*Sighs.*]

Mim. Why, Mr. de Rigby—what a sigh!

Rig. Did I sigh?

Mim. I never heard such a gasp.

Rig. Yes. I am afraid something very serious is going on here. [*Hand on heart.*]

Mim. Heavens! Oh, I see, you're in love.

Rig. I thing it's something like that. What do you say to Miss Barbie?

Mim. [*Clapping her hands.*] Miss Barbie! That's splendid!

Rig. I'm not so sure about that. I havn't asked her yet. She may be gasping for some one else, and not wasting a thought on me.

Mim. Nonsense! A gentleman like you!

Rig. You flatter me. [*Smoothes his hair.*]

Mim. All you have to do is to propose. You can't be afraid to ask her. If you are, why—write.

Rig. Yes, I know. I once knew of a fellow who proposed by telegraph—and another fellow got the lady.

Mim. Shall I try to sound her for you?

Rig. Not for the world, until I've had a chance to make a favorable impression. One may occur to-night, if not, some other time. And yet, suspense is dreadful.

Mim. It is the sweetest thing about love, and the best sign that it's true. Don't you know the words of the song? [*Sings a song without music.*

Supposing a man all wrinkled and old,
  Should come to me jingling his silver and gold,
And offer a share of his Mammon to me
  If I to the sale of myself would agree—
    I wouldn't. Would you?

Suppose that a hero, all bristling with fame,
  And big with the weight of a wonderful name,
Should offer, in a moment of grand condescension,
  To give me his hand a little attention—
    I wouldn't. Would you?

Supposing a youth, with his heart in his eyes,
  That shine like the light of the beautiful skies,
Would promise to love me through all his glad life,
  And beg that I be his own dear little wife—
    Guess I would! Wouldn't you?

Towards the last line, RIG. *places his arm about her waist for an instant and kisses her.*

MRS. PARTADGE *enters,* R. 1 E., *sees the situation, and holds up her hands.*

Mrs. Partradge. Well, upon my word, **Mr.** Duc de Montebello!

Mim. Oh! [*Runs off,* R. U. E., RIG. *starts to* L., *and examines bric-a-brac.*]

Rig. [L.] I am extremely sorry that—

Mrs. P. No apologies are needed. It was quite a romantic picture.

Rig. Yes, it was only a picture. Nothing real about it. Fancy sketch. Perfectly harmless.

Mrs. P. Of course—one of your jokes. [*Going,* R. U. E.] They are all perfectly harmless—deceptions. [*Exits.*]

Rig. Now, that was very unfortunate. But I never saw a person so predisposed to unfavorable views of everything I do. [*Sits*, L.]

BARBIE *enters*, R. 1 E., *in ball dress and high spirits.*

Barbie. I wonder if the guests have come yet. Why, Mr. de Rigby, is that you? What a jolly evening we're going to have!

Rig. [*Gloomily*, L.] Yes, I suppose so.

Bar. You don't seem to be glad.

Rig. No wonder. I'm the victim of bad luck. My whole life is a series of knock downs.

Bar. Do you consider your visit here one of them?

Rig. No, it's one of the few things that set me up again.

Bar. Why, I never dreamt you could be so solemn.

Rig. That's my trouble exactly. People won't understand me. Good sort of fellow, De Rigby! But no depth—no breadth —no height—superficial!

Bar. There must be somebody, who knows you better.

Rig. Nobody takes the trouble to even find out.

Bar. Suppose I have a higher opinion of you?

Rig. [*Seizing her hand.*] If you had, my whole trouble would vanish like smoke.

Bar. [*Withdraws her hand.*] Now you've overdone it! If you had simply taken my hand and said: "I thank you," it would have deepened my impression of your sincerity. But to gush that way—no one could believe it genuine. [*Crosses to* L.]

Rig. [*Aside, dejected.*] It seems there is a false ring about me. She won't believe. Now what is a chap to do?

MIMA *re-enters from* R. U. E.

Mima. Oh, Miss Barbie! Papa's got back, and he says the gentlemen will soon be home. He says they didn't have a bit of luck, and he never saw Mr. Spencer so down-hearted—and he heard him say to Mr. Laurens: "We'd have had a deuced better time at home, old chap;" and Mr. Laurens said: "That's so, old chap"—and they're both coming back. Won't they be surprised at all that's going on! [*Crossing, then sly glance at Rig.; then aside to Bar.*] Isn't he nice, and don't he love somebody? [*Going to Rig.*] Brace up! [*Exits*, R. U. E.]

Rig. [*Starts up, aside.*] Gad, I will.

Bar. You've made quite a friend of her.

Rig. I wanted to make a friend of you! To return to our subject, you were saying—

4

Bar. No, *you* were saying.

Rig. To be sure, I was saying that your opinion—your good opinion—in my opinion, was the only opinion.

Bar. We had got past that.

Rig. Oh, yes; and I was going on to say, that if I loved a girl, nobody could, would, or should love her more, or more truly than I could love her; emphatically, yours truly emphatically, or better or more truly than yours truly.

Bar. [*Slyly.*] And you also complained that no one would believe you?

Rig. We had got past that, Miss Barbie! I assure you that I am much better than my reputation. Try me, you'll find [*Taking her hand.*] you're the only person—beg pardon, I mean party—you're the only girl in the world that—

Bar. [*Withdraws her hand.*] No—here's some one else. [RIG. *makes a bolt up the stairs,* R. C.]

MERYL *enters in ball dress,* L. D.

Meryl. [*Crosses to* C.] Well, have you two had enough of croquet to-day?

Bar. We had quite enough of Auntie's croquet. It's awfully interesting to be watched and signaled at behind a gentleman's back!

FLUTTERBY *enters,* R. C., *evening dress.*

Mer. You ought to pay every respect to her admonitions.

Bar. Now you are prosing. I don't care, I believe everybody's going to have a pick at me. [*Crosses to* L., *flounces up* C., *pouting.*]

Mer. [*Getting* R.] You have lost Wirt's good opinion forever by staying at home to-day, instead of shooting.

Flutterby. [R.] I'm indifferent, if I have yours. [*They go aside,* R.]

Rig. [*Up stage,* C.] He's at it. I must pay attention. I wonder if stocks are up or down?

Bar. [*To Rig.*] What shall we do until the people come? Shall we play something?

Rig. [*Absently, watching others.*] Ye—yes.

Bar. Chess? No—I don't like chess. Backgammon? No, Gobang? Do you play gobang?

Rig. [*Same.*] Yes—oh, yes—with pleasure. [BAR. *brings little table forward, opens drawer and puts out counters, etc.*]

Bar. We can sit over here. [RIG. *brings chairs; places one*

L. *of table.* *Both about to sit on it, bump back to back, bow in apology; same business* R. *of table.* *She sits,* L.; *he eyes her a moment with his glass, then sits* R. *of table.*] This is a nice corner, isn't it?

Rig. Capital place. [*After a glance at Flut. and Mer., he sits, his back to* R. FLUT. *and* MER. *in deep conversation.*]

Bar. Which color will you take? I'll take red and you take blue.

Rig. No, don't give me the blues.

Bar. You can see the red too plainly. You take the red and I'll take the blue. [*Pushes a lot of counters over to him.*] You begin. [*They play.*]

Flut. [*To Mer.*] You don't know how glad it makes me to see you cheerful again.

Mer. We must not take our troubles too much to heart.

Flut. It's the only way to be happy. Complete indifference to all, save those who truly love us.

Mer. [*Looking over to Rig. and Bar.*] They seem to be happy, don't they? [FLUT. *turns to look at Rig., as* RIG. *turns cautiously to look at Flut.; both turn away quickly.*]

Bar. Your play.

Rig. I beg pardon. [*They play.*]

Mer. How do you like the little Boston girl?

Flut. I confess I never gave the matter a thought.

Mer. Oh, fie! Have you no eyes for beauty?

Flut. Not of the school girl sort. [*Talks to her; she smiles.*]

Rig. Well, I— [*Looks slyly round at them.*]

Bar. You're not paying the least attention to the game. I could have beaten you half a dozen times. Are you tired of it?

Rig. [*Turns to her suddenly.*] How can you ask? Don't you think they are very confidential?

Bar. It's none of our business.

Rig. No—of course not.

Bar. Go-bang! Ha! ha! I've won! [*Sorts out pieces on board.*]

Rig. Good gracious! You don't tell me you've go-banged me?

Bar. Shall we have another? You begin again. [*They play again,* RIG. *stealing furtive looks at Flut.*]

Mer. If you are so hard to please, you'll never get a wife.

Flut. I've no intention of marrying.

Mer. You are too fond of your liberty.

Flut. [*Taking her hand.*] There is a grave reason.

Mer. How interesting.

Rig. [*Aside, looking across.*] He seems to be taking advantage of the market.

Bar. Your play. I shall begin to think I'm not pleasant to look at, if you turn your head away so much. [*He doesn't heed, and she looks astonished.*] Well!

Flut. Will you listen, if I confide a secret to you?

Mer. [*Withdraws her hand, rises.*] With pleasure.

Flut. [*Rises.*] Let's go on the porch.

Mer. You have certainly succeeded in arousing my curiosity.

Rig. [*Aside.*] He shan't go out of my sight with her. [MER. and FLUT. *go toward* c.; RIG. *suddenly jumps up and gets a shawl from back of chair,* R., *then calls after Mer.*] Ah, Mrs. Laurens! you have forgotten your shawl!

Bar. What is the matter with him?

Mer. Thank you. [*Puts it on;* RIG. *adjusts it.*]

Rig. May I join you? [MER. *exits without heeding.*]

Flut. [*Severely.*] What are you driving at? Go on with your game.

Rig. And let you go on with your game? Not if I know it.

LIDA *enters,* R. U. E., *in ball dress.*

Lida. Where's Meryl?

Rig. This way! Just on the porch. [*Offers his arm, leads her to* c., *bows her out and returns. To Flut.*] Now *you* can go, too!

Flut. Confound it! [*Exits in a rage,* c.]

Rig. I think I've spoiled that little game.

Bar. I'm pretty sure you've spoiled this one.

Rig. [*Comes down gallantly.*] Now let's begin in earnest. [*He sits at table.*]

Bar. Now—indeed! [*Rises and tosses board over his lap.*]

Rig. I declare, you've go-banged me again!

Bar. You may play with somebody else. I've had enough.

Rig. But, Miss Barbie, please don't! I admit, I did permit my attentions to wander for a moment, but—

Bar. For a moment!

Rig. Well, say two moments, or three moments, but I beg a thousand pardons for it.

Bar. If you think you can offend me, and make it up with sugar plums, as if I were a child, you are very much mistaken. You ought to have told me at first you didn't want to play and preferred Mrs. Laurens.

Rig. I cannot tell a lie.

Bar. Oh, George! Don't try to deceive me. I saw it all, and, in the middle of the game, to jump up and run after her! It's a downright insult.

Rig. Excuse me, you don't understand. Allow me to explain. As we say in Latin, the *locus*—

Bar. It can't be explained. Locus! bah! Hocus-pocus! I can just tell you, it's all over between you and me. As we say in Latin, it's *finis.* [*Exits,* R. 1 E.]

Rig. [*Following.*] Don't say that, Miss Barbie! [*She slams the door.*] Please take that back! My unlucky star! [*Turning away from the door.*] I've lost her. She said it was all over between us. So it must have been getting all right between us, and now I've ruined all. [MUSIC, *cracking of whips, carriages, etc., off* L.]

MIMA *enters,* R. U. E.

Mima. They're all coming at once. Just like these country people.

Rig. Are they coming in here?

Mim. No, they're going to the other door.

Rig. Then I can slip out this way, go home and go to bed. I feel as if I wanted to be alone in my misery. [*Exits,* C. MUSIC *louder.*]

Mim. What fun! They've started the dancing already. [*Shot heard outside.*] Oh! [*Starts.*] What on earth's that? Why, there's Mr. Groobie all doubled up, between Mr. de Rigby and Mr. Blum! What can have happened? And there's his wife in the parlor, waiting for him.

The door, C., *opens and enter* GROOBIE *very much doubled up; his nose black and bloody, assisted by* RIGBY *and* BLUM; *he is in very fancy hunting costume, embroidered game-bag, etc.* BLUM *carries his gun.*

Blum. I vos so sorry. I vish I chood myself, I do.

Groobie. [C.] I wouldn't mind it so much, if it wasn't right in the nose.

Bl. [R.] Dot's easy fixed. You get a wax nose.

Gr. Blow your wax noses.

Bl. Let's get him to de kitchen and wash him off.

Rig. Not a bad hurt, I hope. Let's play the hose on him.

Gr. I don't know. It stings like the devil.

Bl. He would get in de wrong way of dat gun. It was all right, till we was getting out de wagon. Somehow my gun went off, while he was at de wrong end. But he comes all right. I pick out de shot. We take him to the kitchen.

Gr. My wife would insist on my going to shoot. She said I was a sport.

Rig. You are the sport of fortune. [*As they are leading Gr. off, to Bl.*] I say, old fellow, if you make business for the profession this way, you'll get on in the world. [*Exeunt,* R. U. E.]

Mim. O, dear, dear! This is dreadful!

BLUM *re-enters.*

Blum. Mima! Poor Mr. Groobie! He got a bad dose. He got an accident by chooding.

Mim. [L.] Has he been shot in a vital spot?

Bl. Yes, right in the end of his nose.

Mim. How did it happen?

Bl. Oh, de way dey all do. Dere was dangers all round—climbing in and out de wagons, and powder and balls flying round and loaded up to the muzzles, and he got right in front of de muzzle as it was going off.

Mim. [*Crosses to* R.] Oh, dear! Just as the ball is about to begin too.

Bl. I guess Mr. Groobie get all the balls he want.

Mim. But Mr. de Rigby will fix him all right. He was in the army once, and ought to know all about wounds.

Bl. [*Suspiciously.*] I say, Mima, I got a question. Is this Mr. de Rigby going to stay at your house all de time?

Mim. I guess so.

Bl. [L.] Dat man he haunt me like a ghost.

Mim. Don't you like him?

Bl. I don't like him so near you all de time.

Mim. For shame!

Bl. [*Crosses to* R.] I can't help it. He's *so* infernal sweet talker.

Mim. [*Urging him off.*] Don't you talk nonsense. You go and get Mr. Groobie fixed up for the ball. If you don't, we'll be settled and done for! As soon as Mrs. Groobie finds out what you've done—

Bl. She gets me de sack, hey?

Mim. Then we are separated forever.

As they are going, they meet RIGBY, R. U. E.

Mim. Is he all right, Mr. de Rigby?

Rigby. All right, with the exception of his looks.

Mim. What does he want with looks? He's married. [*Exits with* BL., R. U. E.]

Rig. A purely business view. [*Sits on sofa,* R.]

LIDA *enters,* C., *with* MERYL.

Lida. [*Aside.*] There he is.

Meryl. You begin the play.

Lid. It's time. Our lords are on their way back.

Mer. [*Crosses to* R.] The comedy must be well under way before they appear. [*Finger to her lips. Exits,* R. U. E.]

Lid. [*Comes forward.*] Why, Mr. de Rigby! Moping here by yourself? Come, I want you to pay me particular attention all the evening. You must not stir from my side, except to wait on Mrs. Laurens. Come now—can we, as two deserted females, claim this knightly service from you?

Rig. [*Gloomily, rises.*] I am yours unreservedly.

Lid. How dismal! What's on your mind?

Rig. A great many things. But chiefly your esteemed aunt. Whenever I try to be agreeable to your sister, she darts in and cuts me off—to us a mythological simile, like Atropos snipping the thread of life. [*Crosses to* L.]

Lid. Let me suggest a little policy. Flatter the aunt.

Rig. I tried to. But she has, to borrow a chemical illustration, so much acid in her looks that it decomposes my resolution. Yet there's nothing I wouldn't do to gain her good will for the sake of a certain person.

Lid. Why, how sentimental.

Rig. Yes, that's it. I assure you in the most solemn confidence—that I love your sister.

Lid. [*Coldly.*] Then why don't you propose?

Rig. [*Promptly.*] She won't have me.

Lid. How do you know?

Rig. She thinks I'm in love with some one else.

Lid. Whom?

Rig. [L.] It's ridiculous, but don't breath it to a soul, pray. It's your friend, Mrs. Laurens.

Lid. Meryl! [*Aside.*] Good! [*Crosses to* L., *aloud.*] Don't try to undeceive her.

Rig. What?

Lid. Let her think so, for a time. Pay Mrs. Laurens as much attention as you pay me, and be devoted to both of us. I'll answer for the consequences.

Rig. [*Crosses to* L.] I beg you to remember, how serious the consequences may be to me.

Lid. You wish to marry, Barbie?

Rig. Can you doubt it?

Lid. If you are serious you shall. I promise that.

BLUM *runs in, stops on seeing the group.*

Rig. I solemnly, sincerely and truly declare and affirm, that I love her with my heart, my whole heart and nothing but my heart, [*Taking Lid.'s hand.*]

Lid. [*Gives hand.*] I believe you.

Rig. You are an angel. [*Kissing her hand.* BL. *holds up both his hands in horror.*]

Blum. [*Going.*] Anoder one! [*Exits,* R. U. E.]

Lid. What was that?

RIG., *going up, sees* MRS. PARTRADGE, *as she enters,* R. U. E.

Rig. The aunt! [*Retreats.*]

Mrs. Partradge. [*Turning down.*] Lida! Oh, there you are.

Lid. Where's Barbie?

Mrs. P. [*With a savage glance at Rig.*] Barbie is in her room. She is so much indisposed, that she will not come out this evening.

Lid. Why, this is very sudden.

Mrs. P. [*With another glance at Rig.*] Very.

Lid. What's the matter with her?

Mrs. P. [*Third glance, very dreadful, at Rig.*] She had received a shock, which it will take her some time to recover from. [*Crosses to* L.]

Lid. [*Alarmed.*] A shock! [*At a telegraphic sign from* RIG. *she bursts into laughter.*] I see.

Rig. If you will allow me to retire, ladies—

Lid. Give me your arm, Mr. de Rigby. We will go to the company.

Rig. [*Aside, as they go up.*] Is she not, to use a botanical comparison, a perfect Upas! [*Exeunt,* R. U. E.]

Mrs. P. The child has found him out at last, thank goodness!

MRS. GROOBIE *enters,* R. U. E. NAP *follows, places furniture close to the sides, and exits.*

Mrs. Groobie. My dear Mrs. Partradge, I've had such a start. My poor husband has been almost killed.

Mrs. P. Almost killed?

Mrs. G. Hit in the very nose. I don't know how he'll ever be able to dance.

Mrs. P. Well, he don't dance on his nose.

Mrs. G. And by the last person I'd expect to perpetrate such an outrage.

Mrs. P. [*Eagerly.*] By Mr. de Rigby?

Mrs. G. De Rigby? No! That little villain, Blum.

Mrs. P. It's a wonder it wasn't the other. [*Crosses to* R.] He does all the mischief he can. I hate that man.

Mrs. G. Hate him? Why?

BLUM *again enters,* R. U. E., *and pauses on seeing the ladies.*

Mrs. P. He's deception itself.

Mrs. G. I thought Mr. de Rigby was a most amiable and harmless person.

Mrs. P. The very worst that ever lived. He holds nothing sacred. First, he begins by courting my Barbie.

Mrs. G. No harm in that.

Mrs. P. Now Barbie tells me, in an agony of tears, that he has been flirting most outrageously with Mrs. Laurens.

Mrs. G. Gracious! We shall not be safe from him.

Blum. [*Aside.*] I see him myself make some loves with Mrs. Spencer.

Mrs. P. [*Confidentially.*] But that is not all. It was only this very night, in this very room, I found him hugging Mima as tight as he could. [*Crosses to* L.]

Bl. Oh! [*With a cry and a reel, he staggers across to sofa,* R.]

Mrs. G. What are you doing there, sir? Listening?

Bl. [*Choking.*] He was hugging my M-Mima. Oh! Ugh! [*Clutches at his necktie.*] I am choke. [*Bursts into tears.*] Oh, Mima, how could you do so! [*Suddenly fierce, crosses to* C.] I will have satisfactions! I will have blood! [*Rushes out,* C.]

Mrs. P. [L.] What is the matter with the man?

Mrs. G. He's in love with Mima, and has probably overheard us.

Mrs. P. He seems dreadfully excited. [*Goes up and looks off.*]

Mrs. G. You heard what he said. Suppose he should attack Mr. de Rigby, and should kill him.

Mrs. P. [*Leading her towards* R. U. E.] Whatever happens, it will be for the best. Here comes the wretch! Let us leave him to the fate he deserves. [*Exeunt,* R. U. E.]

Passing RIGBY, *who enters,* R. U. E., *with severe glances. He puts his glass to his eye looking after them.*

Rigby. There goes the poisonous Upas and a congenial evergreen! I—I wonder why she has taken such a deadly dislike to me.

Enters MIMA, R. U. E., *sees Rig. and suddenly bursts into tears.*

Mima. Oh, Mr. de Rigby! Oh, heavens!

Rig. [*Glass to his eye.*] Oh, it's you. Excuse me. I'm busy.

Mim. [C. R.] Oh, please don't go. I'm so wretched. Oh, heavens!

Rig. Nonsense.

Mim. Nonsense? Oh, heavens!

Rig. You keep on saying oh heavens in a most absurd manner.

Mim. Oh, my Theobald! Oh, heavens!

Rig. There you go again. Theobald? Is that your young druggist?

Mim. He has gone to kill himself. Oh, heavens!

Rig. Don't be afraid. They never take their own physic.

Mim. Oh, if he should swallow a dose of poison!

Rig. It would probably disagree with him.

Mim. Oh, heavens! He says I'm false to him. You know, Mr. de Rigby, whether I'm false to him or not.

Rig. Allow me, my dear, you are the only competent authority on that question.

Mim. But he suspects yòu! [MUSIC *off.*]

Rig. That's fortunate. Suspicions can be cleared up. Dry your eyes, and go and join the merry throng of dancers. Be happy! Your Theobald shall not take poison. He shall marry you, or I'm a Dutchman and he is not.

Mim. [*Brightening.*] But he's gone off.

Rig. Very good. We'll go after him and find him—and if we can't find him, he shall find us.

Mim. Oh, heavens! [*Exeunt,* R. U. E.]

The MUSIC, *as if prelude to Lancers, strikes up very far off. As it decreases,* BARBIE *peeps in from* R. 1 E., *and, finding the apartment empty, enters in short dress.*

Barbie. [*Dolefully.*] I won't speak to that man again! [*Sits.*] I won't even look at him. No wonder he don't show himself. [*Rises.*] They're dancing in there. How nice the music sounds! I'd give anything to be dancing, too. But I won't. I want to punish myself for ever having been so weak as to listen to that man for a moment. I'm so hungry! [*Looks round.*] I think, Aunty might have sent me something to eat—some cakes. [*Goes to sideboard,* L.] What is this? Eclairs? How delicious they look! [*Takes a bite out of one.*] Oh, nice! [*As she eats she looks over the other things.*] Um! What are these? Oh, the costume favors for the cotillion. [*Takes up one.*] I forgot all about them. I meant to pick out such a lovely one for myself. [*Puts them aside and takes up another eclair.*] That music is lovely. [*Dances to it.*] My favorite lesson at boarding school was the dancing one. I know I always got good marks for that! [*Eating and stealing up to look off*, R. U. E.] What are they dancing now? The lancers —oh, they do it all wrong. [*With childlike liveliness.*] Forward! Now again! Oh, oh, oh! It's awful; they don't know anything about it. I'd be ashamed to dance like that. "Forward, ladies"—"chassee and turn." Oh, one of them nearly fell over. This is the way to do it. "Forward all—again—salute— turn—partners—polka all round. Forward all! Oh! oh! Lida is the worst of the lot. Go on, Lida, go on. Oh, dear, somebody is coming! [*Runs off*, R. 1 E., *and peeps out.*]

NAP *enters*, R. U. E., *takes the tray of bon-bons from the sideboard and exits*, R. U. E.,

Bar. [*Comes forward.*] They're going to pull them now. They've come to that figure. [*Picks up her bon-bon and peeps into room.*] Oh, dear, they ain't doing that right either—you forward two, and back—turn partners and salute—then a waltz

She dances all this, as RIGBY *appears*, R. U. E.

—then forward all. [*She extends her arm, with a bon-bon in her hand.*] Then stop! then present arms! then pull! [*She extends her* R. *hand with a bon-bon.* RIGBY *comes forward and, at the last word, speaks.*]

Rigby. [R.] With pleasure! [*Seizing the other end of bonbon.*]

Bar. Let go!

Rig. Never! [*She pulls and snaps the cracker.*] Why you gobanged me again. May I hope for the honor of your hand for the cotillion?

Bar. After what you have done to me? No, sir!

Rig. [*Seizes both her wrists and pulls her hands away every time she tries to bite the eclairs.*] But listen one moment. I've spoiled your whole evening. I've sent you to your room, cut off your dance and your supper, and made you completely miserable. I don't know how I did it, but it seems I have done it. My success is so astonishing, that I think I'll go home to-morrow. Now do let up on me once. Give me one chance, before I go, and one dance.

Bar. Let me go! [*Breaks away and crosses* R.]

Rig. [*Turning away.*] She must positively hate me. I know she does. I—I feel her hate trickling down my back just like— like—

Bar. [*Aside, at door.*] Can't he see that I'm dying to forgive him? [*Bangs the door open.*] The goose! [*Exits,* R. 1 E.]

Rig. Gone! Not merely going, but positively gone!

SPENCER, LAURENS *and* JACKSON *enter,* C., *in shooting dress.* UNCLE JOYCE *staggers on,* R. U. E., *almost exhausted; sinks on sofa,* R., *fanning himself furiously with handkerchief.*

Spencer. Why, what's going on here?

Uncle. [*In costume.*] They'll dance me to death.

Sp. Dancing? Digby, that's your doing.

Rig. Not at all.

Laurens. Well, they're going it.

Sp. Will somebody be good enough to explain?

MIMA *enters,* R. U. E., *fussily.*

Mima. No time now—come, Uncle! [*Taking his arm, all going,* R. U. E., *except* RIG. *Lines spoken rapidly but neat.*]

Rig. I'm innocent, my dear boy, I'm innocent.

Mim. Come, gentlemen, come take partners. [*Hurries off.*]

Sp. What is the meaning of it all?

Lau. We've got into the wrong house. It's a lunatic asylum.

RIG. *is about to follow, when* BLUM, *white and disordered, bursts in,* C.

Blum. [L.] Ha! You was dere, eh?

Rig. Was I? I believe I was.

Bl. Scorpion!

Rig. My good fellow, go away. This is very unkind, after all I've done to help you. Go away, and give me a chance to help myself. [*Crosses to* C.]

Bl. Helps yourself. Is here anything you don't help your-self to?

Rig. Theobald, I am astonished!

Bl. You are de rich man. You have many flocks. You have taken my von leedle lamb.

Rig. I really havn't time. Good evening! [*Going.*]

Bl. Stop, Mr. Coward. [RIG. *turns and wipes eye-glass calmly.*] We are not through. [*Takes two small packages from his pocket.*] Here are two papers. Dere is a powder in each one. Von is Seidlitz powder and de oder is arsenic.

Rig. [L.]   Be very careful not to mix them.

Bl.   Von is for you—de oder is for me.

Rig. [*Putting his glass to his eye.*]   In that case, I take the Seidlitz.

Bl.   No one can tell vich of dem is the oder.   Choose!

Rig.   Thanks.   [*Takes one and puts it into his vest-pocket.*]

Bl.   When de clock strikes ten to-morrow, von of us vill die—when the clock strikes ten, you take your powder und I take mine.

Rig.   Theobald, you're off your burner—your mind's unhinged.

Bl.   Remember, to-morrow, when de clock he strikes ten! [*Exits,* C.]

Rig. [*Calling after him.*]   Call me, if I oversleep myself! Very well done!   None but the brave deserve the fair!   [*Going,* R. U. E.]

MRS. PARTRADGE *enters in costume,* R. U. E.

Rig.   Can I believe my eyes?

Mrs. Partradge.   I hope so!   Nobody could believe your tongue.

Rig.   You are going to join the cotillion?

Mrs. P.   No, sir!   I'm going to my niece's room, and afford the poor child some little share of the amusement she has lost through you.   Why, Barbie!

BARBIE *enters in costume,* R. 1 E.

Barbie.   Well, aunty, you see I resolved to make a sacrifice of my feelings, for Lida's sake.   [*Crosses to* C.]

Rig. [*Aside in rapture.*]   All is not lost.   [*Advances to her.*] What sacrifice shall I make, in return for all your goodness?

Bar. [*Aside to him, smiling.*]   Lead aunty in, the cotillion is going to begin.   [*Exeunt,* R. U. E.]

All enter to minuet time and step.   Ladies on R. *of partners.*

Mrs. P.—Uncle.	1. Minuet.
Mrs. G.—Groobie.	2. Gavote.
Lady—Gentleman.	3. Country dance.
Lady—Gentleman.	4. Tyrolian.
Mima—Flutterby.	5. Country dance.
Lida—Laurens.	6. Tyrolian.
Meryl—Rigby.	7. Gavote.
Barbie—Spencer.	8. Minuet March.

CURTAIN.

ACT IV.

Same as last: Time, Morning.—The fire is lighted.   There is a screen near it, with a chair on either side of it.

SPENCER *and* LIDA *up centre.*   UNCLE JOYCE *near fire-place, reading, with his lap full of magazines and papers.*   MRS. PARTRIDGE *seated near, knitting.*   BARBIE *up stage.*   MERYL *and* LAURENS *in library.*

Spencer.   [*Coming down with* LIDA.]   Of course we all know Digby's way.   Things seem more than they really are with him. This may be simply a case of appearances.

Lida.   But you say yourself he never left her for a whole day. Why did he not go off with you and her husband?

Sp.   Barbie asked him to stay.

Lid.   And he never paid her the slightest attention while you were gone!   He ran after Meryl all the time.

Sp.   You really think there's something—

Lid.   I do.

Sp.   And danger, too?

Lid.   Remember how susceptible a woman is, when neglected by her husband—how grateful for the least attention.

Sp.   It would be a horrible affair.

Barbie.   [*Coming down,* C.]   What are you two plotting?

Lid.   Barbie, I'm very much engaged just now.

Sp.   On a matter of importance.

Lid.   Will you water my flowers—there's a dear?

Bar.   Will I walk off about my business—there's a dear ! Yes, I will, you turtle doves!   Before I'd be so silly—after being married a whole year !   [*Crosses to* L., *goes up.*]

FLUTTERBY *enters,* L.

Flutterby.   Ah, Miss Barbie—I can't see Mrs. Laurens anywhere.   [*Looks down at others.*]

Bar.   [*Taking his arm.*]   No, you must put up with me just now.   [*Gets watering-pot up* L. C., *and goes off with him.*]

Sp.   [*To* Lid.]   What will come of it?   Laurens gets in a passion so easily.

Lid.   It's his own fault.   His wife is not in the least to blame. [*Crosses to* L., *indignantly.*]

Sp. Nice principles! [*Going* L.]

Lid. [*Aside.*] Wait till your turn comes. [*Goes to Mrs. P.*]

LAURENS *and* MERYL *come down from library, pause a moment and look at Sp.*

Meryl. Don't breathe a word to her husband. [*With affected earnestness.*] Promise me, not to tell him.

Laurens. [*Still eyeing Sp.*] I shall act as circumstances require. You must leave it to me. [*Comes down,* L.]

Sp. [*Perceives Lau., gives a gesture of pity, aside, and then goes to him.*] Good morning, Laurens. [*Tone of sympathy.*]

Lau. [*Same.*] Good morning, my dear friend! [*Shakes his hand twice, very warmly.*]

Mer. [*Aside to Lid., up stage.*] My husband swallowed the bait.

Lid. So did mine. I wonder how they will act.

Mer. Look at them now! Each fancies the other the victim of perfidy and deceit.

Mrs. Partradge. [*Rising to go to Sp., knocks over all Unc.'s papers.*] My dear Paul, when you have a few minutes to spare, I would like to have a little conversation with you. [UNC. *has gathered his papers up again.*]

Sp. In a moment.

Mrs. P. There's no hurry. [*Resumes her seat, and knocks over Unc.'s papers again.*] Oh, pray excuse me! Did I really do that?

Uncle. Umph! [*Aside.*] How can a man read with all this bobbing up and down?

Lau. Oh! ah! Spencer! By the way, how long does your friend Rigby stay? [*Observes him closely.*]

Sp. [*Observing him furtively.*] Eh? About a week.

Lau. That's a long time.

Sp. [*Aside.*] Does he suspect?

Lau. I would not be inconsolable, if I found he had to leave to-day.

Sp. Have you—any—special reason for saying so?

Lau. None that I can explain. Don't ask me. [*Shakes his hand doubly again, then draws back.*] You know me—I let fly at a thing, if I see it. Take aim! Fire! Pst! Bang! [*Again shakes his hand.*] A word to the wise—you understand. [*Confidentially, in his ear, as he crosses* R.] He had better go! [*Aside.*] Poor devil! [*Crosses to* L.]

Sp. [*Aside.*] He does suspect! Poor devil! [*Crosses to* R.]

Lau. [*Aside.*] I've done my duty. [*They catch each other looking furtively and turn away.*] Poor devil!

Sp. Poor devil! [*As he turns he falls over Unc.*] Excuse me, uncle. You wished to speak with me, aunt. [*Takes Unc.'s seat when vacated.* LAU. *joins* MER.]

Unc. Ahem! [*Gathers up everything, crosses to sofa,* L., *sits on the two cushions that are at the end, and falls over.*]

Mrs. P. A word in confidence. Unless you take a very decided step, you will see something terrible happen in your house.

Sp. Bless me—what?

Mrs. P. I can't watch everybody—don't ask me any questions, but get rid of Mr. De Rigby as soon as you can.

Sp. You have noticed something wrong, then?

Mrs. P. I am not blind—if every one else is.

Sp. [*Looks round at Lau., they detect each other and turn away.* MER. *and* LID. *exchange merry glances, and shake fingers in direction of their husbands.*] I can't turn the man out of the house.

Mrs. P. If the thing has been generally noticed, he may as well be sent away. He'll have no fun staying here. I wonder what Barbie thinks of him, by this time. Young girls are unfailing clairvoyants. If he has been attentive to any one else, she's seen it first— Barbie! I want to talk to you. [*Takes her over* L., *to sofa, where Unc. has placed himself.*] Excuse me, uncle.

Unc. [*Rises, gathers up his papers and crosses to* R.] I'm hunted like a hare. [*Sits and reads,* R.]

Sp. Barbie, you're a sensible girl.

Bar. So you've found me out at last. No one can hide anything from you.

Sp. Never mind all that. Come, I want you to tell me frankly what you think of Mr. De Rigby.

Bar. I think as you do. He is utterly unreliable.

Sp. Humph! Whom is he paying attention to just now?

Bar. To whoever is nearest to him. He is really wonderful! [*Rises.*] It makes no difference who it is—he pours out his whole soul to us all. Are all your English friends like that? [*Crosses to* C.]

Sp. There are exceptions.

JACKSON *appears at* C.

Bar. There's Jackson wants to see you. How do you do, Jackson? [*She bumps against Unc.; he comes to front table, scarcely noticing her apology; she helps him to pick up his papers; as he stoops, she puts the paper on his head.*] Did I do that? I beg your pardon. [*Exits,* R. 1 E.]

Unc. This is persecution.

Jackson. Morning, Miss.

Sp. Well, Jackson?

Jack. [R. C.] If you think of shooting this morning, sir, there's some of the hill folks come down that say the birds are thick up in the swales.

Lau. [*Advancing, making a sign to Sp.*] I shall stay at home to-day.

Sp. So shall I.

Mer. [*Sarcastically.*] What, *you*, dear?

Lau. Yes, dear. [*Crosses from her.* SP. *goes up with* JACK.]

Mer. [*As she meets* LID., *in subdued tone of merriment.*] Our plan works.

Lid. [*Same.*] The plot thickens. [*They go up*].

Jack. [*To* SP., *as they come forward.*] I've a sort of a favor to ask of you, sir, and yet I don't rightly know how to do it— and yet it's got to be done.

Sp. Speak out—what is it?

Jack. Couldn't Mr. De Rigby move back into the house here —out of my farm? I wouldn't ask it, only—

Sp. [R. C.] What has occurred?

Jack. [L. C.] Oh, nothing's occurred! Nothing! It's only what's going on. You see, my daughter has been cutting up queer with him—whispering and acting intimate, like, well— [*With a burst.*] It don't do to quarter a weasel in a hen-coop, no way you fix it! [*Crosses to* R. MRS. P. *moves to arm-chair in front of fire.*]

Sp. [*Aside, vexed.*] This is too much! Even Mima can't escape. [*Aloud.*] Leave it to me—I'll see to it.

Jack. Much obliged. That's a great load off my mind. By gorm! I worried when she had that pill-box after her, but I never dreamt of her taking up with this puff-box! She may have her poison mixer if she can't be easy. I know what I've got when I've got him. By gorm! I can handle him. So you'll call off the Britisher, will you, sir?

Sp. Yes—yes. I'll attend to it.

Jack. [*Doubling his fist.*] I had thought of attending to it myself, sir, but the thought struck me, that you could point out to him better than I could. All right, sir! [*Going up, turns and looks at* Lau., *aside.*] So Mr. Laurens won't shoot? All right! What's come over him? I believe they've got to be all puff-boxes and ivory back-combs, every one of them! [*Exits*, C.]

Sp. [*He and* LAU. *exchange looks.*] Digby must certainly go home. But how can I make him understand it? Uncle might do it; at all events, he's the only one can try. [*Crosses and leans over Unc.'s chair.*] Uncle, you must do me a favor.

5

Unc. [*Gathering up his things and going to* c.] Yes, yes—I know.

Sp. [R., *detaining him.*] No, no. [*Bringing him down,* c.] I want you to perform a delicate diplomatic mission with respect to Mr. De Rigby.

Unc. Ask him for something out of his room?

Sp. It's no joke. I'm particularly desirous of having him take his departure to-day.

Unc. So am I—about all of 'em. [MRS. P. *gets down to* R. *of table.*]

Sp. Then you won't mind beginning with *him.* No half measures. He must go!

Unc. Am I to tell him so?

Sp. If you can't make him understand by hints—yes.

Unc. It *is* a delicate business, my boy.

Sp. I appreciate it, and I feel that no one can manage it so pleasantly as you. I have thought of a plan. I'll have a decanter of sherry sent in, and you can ask him to take a glass. He won't be astonished at such an invitation from you, you know! you get him warmed up, and then, in a burst of confidence, after two or three glasses, you out with your suggestion.

Unc. Very good. Send in a bottle of champagne; never mind the sherry. You can't get this boy to drink enough sherry to warm up and burst on.

Sp. Very good. You'll manage him. I see that.

Unc. [*Crosses to* c.] Can't I begin by telling our fair friend over there [*Indicating Mrs. P.*] to go first? [MRS. P. *sees him and comes forward.*]

Sp. Oh, uncle! [*Goes up to Lau.*]

Mrs. P. Ah! ah! a little bird whispers, that you've been talking about me.

Unc. Oh—I assure you—

Mrs. P. Now what was it—a dish seasoned with *sauce piquante?* [*Coquettishly.*]

Unc. [*Gallantly.*] Oh, if you had been served up, it would have been with cream [*Crossing, aside.*] of Tartar! [*Goes to fire-place.*]

Mrs. P. Something could be made of him—if I only had time, but that girl engrosses every moment. [*Exits,* R. 1 E.]

RIGBY *enters, greeting everybody.*

Rigby. Good morning! [*To Sp.*] Not off yet?

Sp. [*Gravely.*] We remain at home to-day.

NAP *enters,* R. U. E. SP. *stops him and gives him an order.* He *goes back and exits,* C.

Rig. But you, Laurens, you don't stay home to-day?

Lau. That's exactly what Laurens intends doing.

Rig. Why, you won't know what to do with yourselves! A day without sport!

Lau. [L.] Not at all. I expect some very good sport. We have scented a fox. [*Crosses to Sp.*]

Rig. No!

Lau. Yes, and we'll dig him out, or burn him out this morning.

Rig. [*Crossing between Sp. and Lau.*] That's capital! I should like to be there.

Lau. [*Slaps him on the back.*] Oh, you'll be there! [*Crosses to* R.]

Rig. Has he been after the chickens?

Sp. Yes, one—a very young and tender chicken.

Rig. You're lucky. They generally go for the old hens, too. [MER. *and* LID. *go up.*] They go for everything. [*Follows the ladies up.*] Did you ever see a fox trapped, ladies? [*Converses with them.*]

Sp. [*To Lau.*] I followed your advice. He shall go to-day.

Lau. And not a day too soon. I know what I say! [*They shake hands and separate.*]

Sp. [*Going to Unc.*] We'll have the coast clear. Hold on to him. He's among the women already.

Unc. All right. [*Calls.*] Eh! Mr. de Rigby! [RIG. *turns short around and bumps against Sp.'s elbow.* SP. *takes Lid.'s hand and leads her away.* LAU. *draws his wife's arm within his own; as they are about to exeunt by different entrances,* C. *and* L. U. E:]

Lau. We needn't be present at the fox digging. [LID. *and* MER. *exchange glances, fingers to lips.*]

Sp. We'll hear all about it afterwards.

Mer. Don't be long, Mr. de Rigby.

Lid. You'll find us in the garden, Mr. de Rigby. [*The husbands hurry them off.*]

Rig. [*Down* C.] Be with you directly.

NAP *enters with tray containing bottle of wine, bowl of ice and glasses.*

Unc. Here boy, set them down here. [*Table,* R.] Have a glass of champagne with me, Mr. de Rigby? I always take something about this time of day. You will, eh?

Rig. With pleasure. [*They sit.* NAP *has opened the wine and at sign from* UNC. *exits,* R. U. E.]

Unc. [*Filling glasses.*] I like a young fellow, who humors an old fellow. I know the boys of to-day don't drink. The boys of yesterday do. I'll be fair, here's a toast: To the boys of to-day! They are the wisest. [*Drinks.*]

Rig. And to the boys of yesterday. They are the best! [*Merely tastes his glass.*]

Unc. [*Aside.*] It goes against me to turn this chap out of doors. [*Aloud.*] Age has its privileges; you won't be offended if I give you a bit of advice. [*Drinks.*]

Rig. I shall be delighted—anything you feel called upon to say, must be profitable.

Unc. [*Aside.*] No. I won't give him advice. What right have I to give him advice? [*Aloud.*] You don't drink. [*Refills his own glass.*]

Rig. After you. I think I know what's coming. That's the way my friends always begin, when they're going to mention a few of my shortcomings.

Unc. Nothing of the sort. You're a capital fellow. But we don't quite understand one another yet.

Rig. But we will. Here's to a better understanding. [*Sips from his glass;* UNC. *empties his.*] Now, tell me what fault have you to find with me.

Unc. I? I havn't any fault to find. [*Refills his glass.*] I'm only what you may call a proxy, and I don't know exactly how to begin.

Rig. Perhaps I can help you! I suspect Paul has been putting you up to this. [*Aside.*] It's the spiteful old aunt! [*Aloud.*] Somebody has told him, of course, that she saw something suspicious. [*Lays his hand on Unc.'s sleeve.*] I admit all appearances, but it's all right. I'm merely playing a little comedy.

Unc. [*Drinks.*] So far, so good. You admit the facts?

Rig. No, I only admit the appearances.

Unc. [*Irritated and beginning to show the effects of wine.*] Now what the devil difference does that make? You want to produce an effect by appearances, and you do it. You produce too much effect. We are all affected.

Rig. That's unfortunate, but you understand perfectly— [*Both drink.*]

Unc. Egad, I should think so. I've been in love! All over in love. With 'em all, all over!

Rig. Not all.

Unc. No, unfortunately. But when I was as young as you— [*Taps him on the shoulder.*] life was one glorious intoxication, in which every ugly woman was a beauty, and every beauty a goddess. [*Drinks.*]

Rig. Just my case now.

Unc. Ha! ha! I could tell a few stories and read you a poem or two! Ha! ha! There was one composed to Rebecca! You didn't know Rebecca? No, it was in 1832. The verses didn't begin to do her justice, yet they were strong. [*Recites:*]

> "Divinely fair—perfection's glass
> Reflects no fairer image."

Rig. Pray, go on, I'm anxious to know what rhyme you got for "image."

Unc. That was a poser. Nothing occurred to me but scrimmage, and so I turned it into blank verse. I'd like to read the whole of it.

Rig. [*Rises, crosses to* c.] So you shall, some morning after breakfast.

Unc. So I could! What a pity, though, that you are going away. [*Begins to grow pathetic.*]

Rig. Oh, I'm not going for some time yet.

Unc. Yes, you are. You are going to-day.

Rig. [*Reassuring him.*] No, I'm not—I am really not.

Unc. We would have had such times together, such feasts of reason! And now you must go! [Unc. *is maudlin drunk.*]

Rig. [*Aside.*] Oh, he's got 'em. [*Irritated.*] You seem to have a sort of monomania about my going.

Unc. No, I've not. I know what I'm saying and I'm sorry for it. [*Falls on his neck.*]

Rig. [*Rising.*] Wouldn't you like a little fresh air? [*Assists him to rise.*] Let's take a walk.

Unc. Perhaps you think it's the wine. You was never more mistaken. I know what I'm talking about.

Rig. Of course.

Unc. You're not angry with me? You don't mind what I said?

Rig. About Rebecca? Oh, no! Quite natural in 1832.

Unc. No, I mean about— [*Motions of departure.*] You understand? [*Falls on his neck.*] Oh, why, why, are you going away? [*Tears himself off, exits* c.]

Rig. He's obstinately bent on that hallucination!

BARBIE *enters,* R., *with some loose flowers which she is arranging in a bunch, and looks about for a ribbon.*

Rig. Ah, Miss Barbie! Alone! Without the deadly Upas —I mean your aunt. What a fortunate thing!

Barbie. Fortunate? [*Looking up from her search.*]

Rig. For me, of course.

Bar. [*Searching.*] I am simply looking for a piece of ribbon to tie my flowers.

Rig. [*Hesitating.*] Could you listen to something I have to say, without its interfering with your exploration?

Bar. [*Suddenly assuming coldness.*] You can save your eloquence for some one, who appreciates it more highly—for Mrs. Laurens, perhaps. [*Going up.*]

Rig. [*Eagerly.*] I—I assure you—

Bar. [*Calmly.*] For Mrs. Laurens, who is in the garden, compelled by your absence to put up with the attention of Mr. Flutterby.

Rig. What? Where? [*Rushes out,* C., *putting on his hat.*]

Bar. Oh! [*Indignantly.*] Oh! oh! [*Throws herself on sofa, commences to laugh hysterically, and then changing to a good cry.*]

Mrs. Partradge enters, R. 1 E.

Mrs. Partradge. Why, Barbie, what's the matter?

Bar. Oh, aunt! My heart is broken.

Mrs. P. Has that villain been talking to you? Has he been pouring his Duc de Montebello champagne into your ears?

Bar. Yes, and I've found him out in all his perfidy. Just as he said he didn't, and he wouldn't and he shouldn't, he—he—he rushed off and did it.

Mrs. P. They all do, darling—they all do. [*Soothing and raising her.*]

Bar. [*As they go* R.] He treats me like a mere wax doll. I never, never could have believed, that any one could tell such bare-faced falsehoods, and I'll never, never believe another man again.

Mrs. P. That's right, my dear. Don't believe and they won't deceive. [Bar. *exits, hysterically, supported by* Mrs. P., R. 1 E.]

Meryl *and* Flutterby *enter,* C. L. *He carries her straw hat and parasol. They walk, as if conversing, from library.* Rigby *enters,* C.

Rigby. I can't find her. I can't find him. I can't find either of them. I say, Miss Barbie—ah, I can't find her now. I've lost them all—what's a chap to do? [*Sits in arm-chair at fire.*]

Flutterby. [L.] There's no one here. I can tell you now, I have waited to find you in that dreamy mood I know so well.

Meryl. You must observe me very closely.

Flut. And I have detected the cause of your melancholy. Whenever your husband seems to treat you with indifference— [*She looks at him*] you look as you have looked this morning. [RIG. *looks, to observe the effect.*] The time will come, when this indifference will become a settled neglect, and your melancholy a settled grief.

Mer. [*Sarcastically.*] That's very dismal. What do you recommend?

Flut. There are men, who would not hesitate to say to you: Revenge this indifference by listening to the vows of another.

Mer. They must be particularly bold men, who would suggest that amusement to me!

Flut. There is one who, to gain a smile from you, would stop at nothing.

Mer. Where?

Flut. In this very house.

Mer. Indeed?

Flut. [*Looking round and then in an agitated voice.*] You will know him by the persistence with which he follows you everywhere—haunts you like your shadow and leaves every occupation to fly to your side—in a word, testifies in every motion, the profoundest love. [RIG. *peeps over again and subsides.*] Shall I tell you his name?

Mer. [*Rises.*] No. I think I know him. It is not you, is it Mr. Flutterby?

Flut. [*Staggered by her glances.*] I—I did not refer to myself.

Mer. [*Sarcastically.*] Oh, no! Of course not! But if you did—or if I had to give the *gentleman* an answer, I should tell him it was none of his business, whether my husband treated me well or ill; that no man had a right to criticise a husband's conduct in his wife's presence—and if he persisted, he would be treated as her worst enemy.

Rig. [*Sotto voce.*] Bravo!

Flut. [*Seizes her hand.*] I thank you for these words. Now I'm happy.

Mer. [*Rises.*] I'm afraid you did not quite understand what I said.

Flut. Oh, yes, I did.

Mer. Then bear in mind, that I meant it to apply to every person who pretends to be— [*Pause.*]

Flut. Pretends to be what?

Mer. Fonder of me [*Crosses to* L.] than my husband! Bye-bye. [*Exits,* R. 1 E.]

Flut. [*For a moment very smiling, follows down, turns and sees* RIG., *who laughs at him—sinks back on sofa.*] Devil take it!

Rig. [*Looking at him stoically from his chair.*] Can you tell me the last quotations in connubial stocks?

Flut. Were you there all the time?

Rig. Heard every word of it.

Flut. I've been an ass. [*Starting up,* C.]

Rig. You have.

Flut. Women are the most ungrateful— I think I shall go home to-day.

Rig. I'm going, too. We'll start together.

Flut. It's been a short visit.

Rig. Too long for my luck. I've been treated— [*Pause.*]

As MERYL *re-enters, she pauses as she sees Flut.*

Flut. [*Embarrassed.*] A-a- good morning! [*Slapping his forehead.*] An ass! [*Exits quickly,* C.]

Rig. [*Energetically.*] I must ask your pardon for an indiscretion. I happened to overhear your conversation with our friend.

Meryl. Oh, I don't mind. [*Crosses to* R.]

Rig. And I want to come in for my share of the scolding. I've been haunting you like your shadow, too. But it was to keep that other party off.

Mer. You meant well.

Rig. [R., *sighs.*] Yes, I thought more of your interests than my own. I'm like the dog with the bone—lost what I had in trying to reach after a shadow. [*Stage,* R.]

Mer. Indeed? And what did your bone consist of?

Rig. Something that will never be bone of my bone and flesh of my flesh, I'm afraid.

Mer. This begins to be interesting.

Rig. I have succeeded in convincing Miss Barbie that I am wholly destitute of truth and honor.

Mer. You shall have an opportunity for a full understanding with Barbie, and without interruption. My room is the very place. [*Opens door,* L.] Wait for me in here.

Rig. I'm afraid it's too late. I have a sinking of the heart. [*Exits,* L. 1 E.]

Mer. [*Calling after him.*] You'll find camphor on the table. [*Shuts door.*] I'll have this little knot unravelled in no time. I owe it to him.

SPENCER *re-enters*, C., *looks at her suspiciously.*

Spencer. Pardon my question—have you seen Mr. De Rigby?

Mer. He was here just now. He's going away to-day, and has been [*Handkerchief to eyes, in affected sorrow.*] taking leave of me. [*Crosses to* R.]

Sp. I'm glad of it. You must feel that it is the best for him to go.

Mer. [*Same.*] Yes—oh, yes! [*Bursts out weeping, then laughing to herself, as she exits,* R. 1 E.]

Sp. Unfortunate woman! Her grief will betray her.

UNCLE *enters*, L. U. E., *in festive hilarity, his hat on one side, pink note-sheet in his hand.*

Uncle. Now, my dear boy. [*Looks round.*] Where is he? Where is the boy?

Sp. [R.] De Rigby, uncle? He's packing up.

Unc. [L.] What a pity he's going! Why must he go? [*Cheerfully and changing tone.*] I rummaged among my old papers and found those verses of mine to Rebecca [*Kisses the paper.*] and two or three other poems. He likes 'em; I got 'em for him. [*Gravely.*] That was a delicate commission you gave me—to tell a man to leave your house!

Sp. You succeeded admirably. He's going.

Unc. Is he? Do you know I fancied that I failed to make him understand.

Sp. Not a bit of it.

Unc. I must have managed very cleverly. You know I didn't tell him out and out, to go.

Sp. He took the hint. That was all that was necessary.

Unc. It was the champagne did it! Wonderful thing that wine is! Made everything clear to him, and mixed me up completely. [*Going to* C., *shaking his head.*] I want to read him this poem before he goes. [*Exits,* C.]

Sp. I wonder if Laurens knows he's going? Poor devil! he is in his room, I suppose, trying to smother his jealousy. I'll have him out and— [*Goes to* L. 1 E., *and knocks.*]

RIGBY *opens the door and puts out his head.* SP. *and he look at each other.*

Rigby. [*Finger to lips.*] Sh! don't say anything. [*Retreating.*]

Sp. [*Drawing him out.*] By heavens! Man, what are you doing in that room?

Rig. Don't shout it out.

Sp. I thought you were going away.

Rig. I can't go, till I see Mrs. Laurens.

Sp. What?

Rig. [*Going towards door.*] She told me to wait for her in there.

Sp. Are you mad? Do you know what you are doing?

Rig. My dear fellow, do you know what you are doing? You are acting in the wildest manner.

Sp. Don't mind me. Come, I'll get you out of the way. [*Dragging him up,* R.]

Rig. [*Breaking away and coming down.*] But I tell you I must see her. I promised her I'd wait.

Sp. [*Agitated.*] But not in there! If Laurens found you together! Here, [*Runs to door,* R. U. E.] get in my room; remain quiet, until I bring the wagon to take you to the train. [*Pushes him in* R. D.]

Rig. [*Putting his head out.*] Will you kindly explain at the earliest possible moment?

Sp. Yes, yes! But not now—not now. [*Looks round.*]

Rig. Not now, of course, in your present incoherent state. But I say, old fellow, I must take my leave of Mrs. Spencer—I can't go without that.

Sp. I'll send her to you. Do go in! [*Shuts door.*] How providential that I happened in at the very moment.

LAURENS *enters from library.*

Sp. A minute later and the explosion would have taken place.

Laurens. [L.] Where is the fox—gone to cover?

Sp. [*Eyeing him.*] Yes—he concluded to run.

Lau. [*Quickly.*] Has he really gone?

Sp. He asked me to say good-bye for him.

Lau. Thank heaven! If he had stayed the day out, I believe I should have exploded. [*Crosses to* R.]

Sp. [*Aside.*] I thought so. [*Aloud.*] We are all glad, of course. [*Aside.*] If I only had him safe out of this. I must find Lida. [*Aloud.*] Shall we join the ladies? They must be expecting us. [*Going up,* C.]

Lau. [*Taking out cigar-case.*] Yes, as soon as I light a cigar. [*Going to fire.*]

Sp. [*Looking off.*] Ah, there's Lida! [*To Lau.*] Come along. [*Exits,* C.]

As Lau. *strikes a match,* Rigby *cautiously peeps out of door,* R.

Lau. Presently. [*Sees Rig., flings match one way and cigar another, runs up and looks off,* C., *then comes down in perturbation.* Rig. *puts up his glass, to inspect Lau.'s movement.*] I thought you were gone!

Rig. [R.] I suppose there's no particular hurry.

Lau. [*Anxiously.*] What are you waiting for?

Rig. I'm waiting for Mrs. Spencer.

Lau. Unhappy wretch! And in her own room!

Rig. [*Coming out.*] But Mrs. Spenc—

Lau. [*With a bound closes his mouth with his hand.*] Sh! [*Looks round.*] Have you not thought of the consequences? Spencer is half mad already.

Rig. So I thought. Do you know what's the matter with him?

Lau. Can't you guess?

Rig. Havn't the remotest notion.

Spencer. [*Outside.*] Laurens!

Lau. [*Alarmed, seizing Rig.'s arm and dragging him to* L.] Here he comes! He must not see you here!

Rig. No? Well, I'd better go in. [*Goes to* R.]

Lau. Not there! not there! Conceal yourself!

Rig. But, my dear fellow—

Lau. For heaven's sake, man, listen to reason! Be guided by me. Avoid Spencer, until you can slip out unobserved.

Spencer. [*Outside.*] Laurens! Arn't you coming?

Lau. [*Drags Rig. to* L. 1 E., *and opens door.*] Get into my room, and don't utter a word.

Rig. [*In the room, putting his head out, and deliberately.*] I say, Laurens, are you sure you know what you're doing?

Lau. [*Has come* C.] Perfectly.

Rig. Thank you. In that case I'm quite satisfied. We are now in *status quo.*

Lau. [*Shutting door on him.*] It's all right I tell you.

Spencer *enters* C., *looks at* Lau. *then at* R. 2 D.

Spencer. I thought you were coming.

Lau. [*Picks up newspaper from sofa.*] I stopped to look at the papers.

Sp. [*Aside.*] Reading it upside down.

Lau. Don't let me keep you. [*Rises.*]

Sp. [*Sits by fire and takes up paper.*] No. I merely wish to begin something I finished this morning.

Lau. [*Aside.*] Last Sunday's Herald! I wish he'd leave. [*Looks at door,* L.]

Sp. [*Aside.*] What keeps him here? [*Glances at door,* R. *Aloud.*] Beautiful day out of doors.

Lau. [*Yawns back to sofa.*] Don't care for it much. [*Aside.*] Why don't he go out, and enjoy it?

Blum. [*Outside.*] Where is he? Where is he?

Sp. Hark! What's that?

Bl. [*Outside and nearer.*] Where is he? Let me find him!

SPENCER *and* LAURENS *start up, as* BLUM *bursts in, holding an empty tumbler in one hand and a stomach-pump in the other, and very much disordered.*

Blum. Where is he? Is he dead?

Sp. Who? What? What is the matter?

Bl. [*Falls backward,* LAU. *and* SP. *pick him up. He gazes wildly from one to the other.*] Is he very dead?

Sp. What are you gasping about?

Bl. Where is Mr. De Rigby?

Sp. and Lau. [*Looking at each other.*] I don't know.

Bl. Oh, gentlemen, hunt him up. He is a dead man. I have the Seidlitz powder. He got the arsenic.

Sp. What is it?   } [*Together.*]
Lau. Nonsense.   }

Bl. It's past ten o'clock. I swallowed my powder as de clock he was striking. It was enough. The taste he was Seidlitz. But at dat moment, vere was he? He was taking pizzin. In two hours he is a dead man. Help me find him. It's not too late, I've brought everything. Here is a stomach-pump. Oh my legs. he give way. [*Sinks down, as they hold him. He has turned face up stage.*]

Sp. [*Seizes Bl.'s arm.*] We'll hunt him up.

Lau. [*Seizes other arm.*] We'll find him. [*Aside.*] How lucky!

Sp. [*Aside.*] A good excuse.

Bl. I pump him out in no time. [*He is carried off,* C., *between the two.*]

Rig. [*Puts his head out quickly as they go off,* C.] They evidently think the little Dutchman a lunatic, and he's the only sane man of the three. Perhaps there's a plot to mystify me. This hiding me in one room and then in another. By Jove, I begin to have enough of it, and the first person I meet is likely to find me a decidedly unpleasant customer.

BARBIE *and* MERYL *enter*, R. 1 E.

Barbie. Mr. De Rigby! [*Timidly.*]
Rig. [*Turns savagely, then changing.*] I—I make a exception in this case.
Bar. [C.] I understand you are about to leave us.
Rig. It appears I can be spared without inconvenience around here.
Bar. You are angry. It's partly my fault.
Rig. Yes, I can't deny that. [MER. *goes up.*]
Bar. Everything has been explained by Mrs. Laurens, and I owe you an apology.
Rig. Thank you. I'm not quite perfect, but when I spoke to you, I meant every word I said.
Bar. I know that—and so, in token of reconciliation. [*Gives her hand.*] Let's part in peace.
Rig. I don't think there's any hurry about my going to-day. You are going to stay, are you not?
Bar. Oh, yes, for some time.
Rig. That'll give me time to—to tell you—hem—tell you— [*Crosses to* R.]
Bar. What? [*Pretending innocence.*]
Meryl. To tell you that he loves you! [*Darts out,* C.]

As MRS. PARTRADGE *enters,* R. U. E.

Rig. Yes, that's it. [*Takes her hand impulsively.*]
Mrs. Partradge. Ah!
Bar. [*Struggles with Rig.*] Let me go.
Rig. Did you hear what she said?
Mrs. P. I heard what she said, sir.
Rig. Then please hear, what I say. I love your niece. [*To Bar.*] Won't you believe me now? [BAR. *turns away.*]
Mrs. P. Barbie, I'm surprised! Give him his answer!
Bar. [*Throws her arms impulsively round Rig.'s neck.*] There!

SPENCER *and* LIDA *enter,* C.

Mrs. P. Oh! [*With a shriek, she falls into Sp.'s arms.*]
Spencer. What's the matter? Why, aunt, don't give up like that.

MERYL *and* LAURENS *enter,* C.

Mrs. P. [*Down* L.] She's lost! To throw herself into the

arms of the Duc de Montebello—a frivolous, foolish, good-for-nothing!

Bar. Oh, he's a real nice little fellow, aunty!

Sp. Stop! I can't hear another word. If there has ever been a misjudged man in the world, it's Rigby. [*Takes his hand.*]

Laurens. A truer friend never breathed. [*Takes his hand.*]

BLUM *entering, with* MIMA *at back.*

Blum. Vere is he! Dere he is! Alive and shaking! Even poison can't kill him! [*Comes down and shakes both hands.*] She tole me all, and her farder he say rader dan you to have her, he trow her away to me. [MIM. *pulls him away.*] Dot was all right. [*Crosses with* MIM. *to* R. C.]

Mima. We owe him all the happiness of our lives, and if I dared to kiss him— [BAR. *crosses to* Rig.]

Rig. Please don't. This is harder to stand up against than a knock down.

Bar. They all see you, now, as I do.

UNCLE *enters,* C., *quickly.*

Uncle. Not a sign of him anywhere! [R. *sees* Rig.] Ah, there you are! Been looking for you everywhere. I've got— [*Shows poems, then pauses, and suddenly with emotion.*] It's a confounded pity, you've got to go to-day.

SP. *plucks him by the sleeve, and frowns and shakes his head.* LID. *and* MER. *both put their hands over his mouth, and shake their heads.*

Unc. Eh? No?

Sp. No.

Lida. No.

Meryl and Lau. No.

Unc. No! Well, you needn't go then. I'm glad of it. We are all glad of it, aren't we?

All. Yes, yes!

Unc. And you can stay with us as long—as long as— I say, how long shall he stay with us?

Bar. Why, as long as ever our old friends on the other side of the footlights will come and welcome our foreign friend on this side of them.

CURTAIN.

www.ingramcontent.com/pod-product-compliance
Lightning Source LLC
Chambersburg PA
CBHW030006030726
47499CB00008B/2919